THE
DOUBLE
DISAPPEARANCE
OF WALTER FOZBEK

Other Avon Camelot Books by
Steve Senn

RALPH FOZBEK AND THE AMAZING
BLACK HOLE PATROL

STEVE SENN was born in Americus, Georgia, and grew
up in a small southern town whose main industry was
producing peanut butter. He attended Ringling School of
Art in Sarasota, Florida, and has lived in Key West and
Miami. Today he lives in Jacksonville, Florida, with his
wife and son and works as an illustrator for the *Florida-
Times Union Newspaper.*

Steve Senn is also an author-illustrator presently living in
the Dinosaur World. He is the same kind of person as the
Human one listed above, but he is a Triceratops.

THE DOUBLE DISAPPEARANCE OF WALTER FOZBEK

Written and Illustrated by
Steve Senn

AN AVON CAMELOT BOOK

For Ron Gordon,
who introduced me to dinosaurs

7th grade reading level has been determined by using the Fry Readability Scale.

AVON BOOKS
A division of
The Hearst Corporation
1790 Broadway
New York, New York 10019

The Hastings House edition contains the following
Library of Congress Cataloging in Publication Data:

Senn, Steve.
 The double disappearance of Walter Fozbek.

 SUMMARY: Walter wakes one ordinary summer morning and
discovers he has somehow been catapulted into a world populated by
dinosaurs.
[1. Dinosaurs—Fiction.   2. Space and time—Fiction]   I. Title.
PZ7.S475Do   1980   [Fic]   80-23857

First Camelot Printing: March 1983

CAMELOT TRADEMARK REG. U.S. PAT. OFF. AND IN
OTHER COUNTRIES, MARCA REGISTRADA, HECHO EN
U.S.A.

Printed in the U.S.A.

OP 10 9 8 7 6 5 4 3 2

Contents

1   A Very Different Summer Morning   7

2   Into the Dinosaur World   15

3   Dr. Krebnickel   28

4   Quarwyn   37

5   The Black Hole   44

6   The Barrier   49

7   The Riddle of Return   55

8   The Search   66

9   Panic in the Park   75

10   Dr. Heminglas   84

11   The Missing Ingredient   93

12   A Reducing Course   102

13   Back Again   108

14   The Dinosaur Festival   116

1 : A Very Different Summer Morning

WHEN Walter woke up he didn't notice anything different. It was a Saturday in early July, and on summer mornings he liked to lie in bed and enjoy not having to go to school. He wiggled his toes down deeper in the covers where the sheets were cool and watched early morning streamers of sun flow in the window. His cousin Ralph's room looked just like it had always looked. He had been visiting Ralph for the whole week while his parents were on vacation, but they were due back tonight. Walter began planning the things he and Ralph could do on their last day. First they would watch some TV cartoons, maybe Tarzan . . .

Then he noticed something. Somebody had taken down Ralph's Hank Aaron Breaks the Record poster and put up one just like it, only with a huge green Dinosaur swinging the bat. The Dinosaur had on a Hank Aaron baseball uniform, and the poster even had Hank Aaron's name in the same big orange lettering on it. Walter sat up in bed. He blinked. He couldn't figure out how they managed to fake a picture of a Dinosaur in a baseball uniform. It must be a joke Ralph was playing on him.

Trying not to wake Ralph, Walter reached over and got a Superman comic from the stack on Ralph's desk to read before breakfast. He blinked again. The bold red letters at the top of the comic read: SUPER-SAUR. And it had a picture of a muscular flying Tyrannosaur fighting a spaceship on the cover. He leafed through it in amazement. All the people had turned to Dinosaurs. Lois Lane was a pretty duck-billed Dinosaur. Jimmy Olsen was a punk Stegosaur with orange spines. And Perry White was a gruff old horned Triceratops. The rest of the comic books were like that, too. Walter knew Ralph had a strange sense of humor, but this was very weird. How could he have gotten Dinosaurs in all his comic books? There was even a Dinosaur Conan the Barbarian!

Feeling sort of scared, Walter leaned out of bed and nudged the corner of Ralph's bed with his toe.

"Ralph! Wake up," he whispered.

Ralph snorted. Walter finally had to kick the bed. After some wriggling around in the covers, Ralph sat up. Walter yelped. There was a Triceratops in Ralph's pajamas! And it looked like Ralph! Ralph's beak dropped wide open when he saw Walter. Then Ralph yelped.

They both dove to different parts of the room. Walter ended up teetering on top of a bookcase and the only part of Ralph that was visible was a stubby grey tail beneath the bed. Then, slowly, a horn emerged, pushing the fallen sheets aside. When the little yellow Dinosaur eye peered out at him, Walter couldn't help it, he yelped again. That frightened Ralph so much he thumped his head against the bottom of the bed and howled. Walter lost his footing then and fell off the bookcase and knocked over Ralph's telescope.

From downstairs Ralph's mother called up, "Stop horsing around, boys, and get dressed! Breakfast will be ready soon!"

The sound of Aunt Alice's voice calmed Walter down some.

"R-Ralph, is that you under the bed?" he said.

"Uh, yes. Walter?"

"I'm okay. But what happened to you?"

"Me!" Ralph gasped, crawling out from under the bed. "What about you—you're all pink! And where are your horns?"

"I don't have any horns," Walter said, "but you sure do!"

"Only three," said Ralph, checking them with his stubby paw.

"Only three! Good grief, Ralph, you're a Dinosaur!"

Ralph laughed a strange squeaky laugh. "Isn't everyone?"

"I'm not," Walter whimpered, glancing at his hand just to make sure. "How long have you been like that?"

"All my life," Ralph said. "Are you sure you're my cousin Walter? If you are something awful has happened."

Ralph stood up. He was definitely wearing the same yellow pajamas he'd had on the night before, except they now had a sleeve in back for his short tail.

"You mean my parents are Dinosaurs?"

"Sure. Everybody is a Dinosaur. Nobody looks like you. You look like an exhibit at the museum. There are fossils from a million years ago that look a lot like you."

Ralph handed him the "H" encyclopedia and told him to look up Humans while he got dressed. The book was round, and bound in rough pebbly grey leather. As he flipped through, Walter felt sort of queasy to see so many photographs of Dinosaurs. Sam Houston was a Triceratops. Wild Bill Hickok was an Ankylosaur. Warren Harding was a presidential Trachodon. The going got queasier when he reached Humans. All the pictures of people like he knew were artists conceptions drawn from fossils. There was a fossil of a man in a business suit and an impression in some sandstone of a glove. The article said that the last true Humans had died out over a million years ago.

"There are no people here," Walter whimpered, beginning to realize something was very wrong.

"What do you mean? I'm a people. So are your parents."

"My mother and father are Humans. These are Dinosaurs!"

"But they're still people," Ralph insisted.

Just then there was a rap at the door and Ralph's mother said, "Time for breakfast, boys."

Walter panicked. "What am I doing in this crazy Dinosaur world? How am I going to get back? I want to be where everyone is Human and Dinosaurs are the ones who are extinct!"

"Look," said Ralph sharply, trying to be calm, "I don't think we're going to solve this before breakfast. The only one who can help us is Dr. Krebnickel."

"Dr. Krebnickel," Walter repeated. "Y-You mean you know Dr. Krebnickel? But he's Human."

"Not the one I know," Ralph snorted. "He's a normal Trachodon."

Walter felt a little calmer. If anyone could help him it would be Dr. Krebnickel, even a Dinosaur Dr. Krebnickel, though the thought made him shudder. The doctor was a great scientist; he had a wonderful laboratory, built almost entirely from odds and ends collected from around the world. And although he was very sloppy and rather poor, and other scientists called him a quack, Dr. Krebnickel was one of the nicest people Walter knew. It made Walter feel a little safer to think of him.

"But how do we get to his house?" Walter gulped, suddenly remembering his problem.

Ralph's shoulders sagged. "If you go downstairs looking like that, my folks will flip out. We've got to do something!"

They decided that a disguise was their only way to get out of the house without a general panic. Somehow Walter had to look like a Dinosaur. Ralph helped Walter into his Dinosaur clothes. They were a little large and had a tail sleeve, and they were thick and rough, but they stayed on all right. Next Ralph got his Triceratopsian football helmet (which was shaped like a Triceratops head, of course) and put it on Walter. Then he began smearing grey modeling clay all over it.

"Yeccchhh!" Walter said.

"Stop complaining," Ralph said sternly. "We've got to make you look like you used to. That's the only way we are going to get anywhere. If grownups get involved we'll never be able to get to Dr. Krebnickel."

Walter gulped as a sudden memory iced his heart. "Ralph, my parents are coming for me tonight. If I'm a freak to them . . ."

"We'd better get to Dr. Krebnickel's," was all Ralph would say.

He stood still while Ralph modeled a horn for his nose and one over each eye. They put on winter mittens, Triceratops shaped, and painted them with some poster paint, and made a tail from construction paper and pinned it inside his pants. Ralph used crayons for the finishing touches. His shoes they filled with crumpled up comic books until they fit. Walter hated to see Supersaur put to such a use.

"It'll have to do," Ralph said finally.

"Do you think they'll be fooled by all this?"

Ralph shrugged. "You know how preoccupied parents always are. Maybe they won't notice. If they discover you, we'll just have to keep them calm. Here," he said, putting a wad of clay and some crayons in Walter's shirt pocket. "We may need these later for touch-ups." He patted Walter reassuringly. "Now, whatever happens, don't freak out."

As Ralph opened the bedroom door, Walter crossed his fingers inside his mittens. He gulped and followed his cousin out the door.

Walter freaked out.

2: *Into the Dinosaur World*

THE house was a Dinosaur house. Walter had not noticed it so much in Ralph's small room, but now he realized how alien everything was. It was as though someone had gone through his Aunt Alice's house and redesigned everything with Triceratopses in mind.

He took a timid step backwards but Ralph grabbed his mittened hand and tugged.

"C'mon, Walter," he insisted. "What's the matter?"

Walter knew what the matter was, but he couldn't speak.

The carpet that yesterday had been a blue shag was now a grey pebbly tile. It was like walking on an alligator's back. Everything in the house was shorter and fatter. There were lots of thick green jungle plants

15

in pots. All the corners in the house were rounded and the air seemed moist.

Suddenly a horrid little creature ran out of a nearby room, squealed, and paused in front of Walter.

"Walter looks funny," it giggled, then thumped on with small elephant steps down the stairs.

Good grief! It was his little cousin Dolly, hateful as ever and twice as ugly, with a stumpy brown horn over each eye instead of curls.

"Don't worry about her," Ralph whispered as they descended, "No one pays her any attention."

He followed Ralph downstairs. Everyone was already at the table. He shuddered. Uncle Albert was big. No, actually, he wasn't any taller, but he was certainly wider. Probably since he didn't have to go to work today, he wore an undershirt bunched around his thick grey arms. He was reading the newspaper. The only part of his face Walter could see were two horns bobbing over the paper. But that was all Walter wanted to see.

Aunt Alice hurried in with a steaming plate of some sort of broad leaves. She too was wider and chunkier, though no taller than his Human aunt. Instead of dark hair, she had a big lumpy grey frill around her face, but somehow she definitely resembled his own aunt.

Walter seated himself carefully in a blocky chair so that his tail went into the proper hole. Dolly sat across from him. She stuck her warty brown tongue out at him when Aunt Alice turned away. Walter shuddered again.

"Turn off that dratted TV, Ralph," Uncle Albert groused. "I can't stand the noise while I'm eating."

Ralph ran into the living room. The television sat on fat legs beside a couch upholstered in thick bumpy leather. With a start Walter recognized the opening credits for the TV show just as Ralph turned it off. It had been *Saurzan of the Jungle*. A sleek Dryptosaur on a vine swung past the lettering before the picture faded.

Uncle Albert folded back his paper and began eating as Aunt Alice poured him some more coffee.

Walter tried not to think about what he was eating. The brown strips looked like bacon but didn't taste like it. It was difficult getting the toast underneath his clay beak. And he worried that someone would notice the strange way he was holding his Triceratops fork lumped up in the painted mittens. But no one seemed to pay any attention. Uncle Albert was still reading and his aunt was helping Dolly find her toast with the jelly knife.

"You're looking pale, Walter. Be sure to eat all your bird strips," was the only thing she said.

So that was what the bacon was.

Walter felt queasy. How could he be calmly eating breakfast with a family of Dinosaurs? What was going on?

"The armored Dinosaurs are planning another railway strike," Uncle Albert read over the front page of the newspaper. He was sort of a news buff, but mostly he enjoyed grumbling about things. He complained loudly about the armored Dinosaurs. Especially the Ankylosaurs, who were a bad lot according to him.

"But—you're all Dinosaurs," Walter almost said in amazement. But he caught himself in time. He stirred his leaves absent-mindedly.

"Eat up, Walter," Aunt Alice reminded him in a rather nasal voice, "I don't want your mother to accuse me of starving you."

Walter quickly lowered his head and stuffed some leaves in his mouth, but he couldn't taste them. His parents! He didn't want to see them in a Dinosaur condition. Besides, how could he be sure they would still love him? He didn't want to see any more Dinosaurs at all.

He and Ralph finished breakfast at the same time and excused themselves from the table. Ralph told his mother they would be at the playground in Teehalt Park.

"You're kidding," she replied. "I thought you kids were addicted to *Saurzan* on Saturday mornings."

As they passed the bricabrac stand in the hall, Walter noticed something. Gooseflesh wrinkled underneath his disguise. Dolly's bronzed baby shoes were gone, and in their place was a shiny bronzed eggshell as big as a grapefruit.

He followed Ralph out of the oddly wider front door into the Dinosaur world.

He gulped. Everything was the same, only different. The same street ran by Aunt Alice's, but the

houses on it were squarer, blockier. Their corners were more rounded, and eaves sometimes wore long horned points like oriental houses. Roofs were shingled with round horny plates in rows like the scales on a lizard.

"What's wrong now?" Ralph demanded irritably and walked back to where Walter stood paralyzed.

Walter shook his head. "It's true. It really is. I'm in a Dinosaur world. There's Hipps Road just like yesterday, and there's Mr. Bledsoe watering his lawn. Only now he's a . . . Corythosaur. Everything is just like it was before, except it's made for Dinosaurs."

A big spiny truck whizzed by them honking a blaring Dinosaurian horn that sounded like Godzilla gargling. Then the police car squealed past them after the truck. The siren was a horrible warbling growl.

Walter shook his head. "At least I know my way around. All the details, like houses and streets and people's names are the same."

They turned down Hipps Road through the suburbs to the old section of town where Dr. Krebnickel lived. They had to go behind Wuffstead Memorial High School and pass through Teehalt Park. The park was filled with every variety of young Dinosaur playing on the swings or the slides. Their cries of glee were a lot like Humans', except in a rather grunting sort of way.

As they ran, Walter tried not to stare at the Tyrannosaur policemen with their Stegosaur-spiked clubs, or the other Dinosaurs in their horned and leathery cars. The clay on his face was beginning to get hot and slippery.

At last they turned down Mars Road and Walter was relieved to see Dr. Krebnickel's house, with just a few dinosaur alterations, standing where it always had. It was a very old one at the top of a hill, and it was completely shaded by a giant oak in front and a billboard behind it. Only a single turret of the house rose through the tree's branches into the sky. It was the room Dr. Krebnickel used as an observatory. The house was sandwiched between two dark houses. Where Walter came from old women lived in them. Sometimes the old ladies would sit on their porches and scowl at Walter and Ralph. He was glad to see they weren't out today.

In front of the house, at the top of the steps was a weathered sign that read: PROFESSAUR LADISLAV KREBNICKEL, METALLURGIST, PHYSICIST, ALCHEMIST, AND INVENTOR.

Breathlessly, they arrived at Dr. Krebnickel's door and Walter turned the brass crank to the doorbell. Now it was shaped like a twisted horn, but the chimes, which were the formula for hydrochloric acid converted to music, sounded the same as always. Walter held what breath he'd finally caught and watched the lace curtains at the windows in the door. He sure hoped Dr. Krebnickel could fix everything.

But nothing stirred the lace curtains. No footsteps

echoed in the house in answer to the chimes. Nothing. Ralph grabbed and twisted the doorbell again. The odd chemical music tinkled, but the house was silent.

Walter felt his Human heart bobbing lighter and lighter up his chest. Where was Dr. Krebnickel?

Suddenly, about the fifteenth time Ralph desperately turned the chimes, an angry voice startled them.

"You there! Stop that racket! What do you want!?"

They whirled to find an old lady leaning out of an upper balcony next door. She was one of the busybody neighbors who were always pestering Dr. Krebnickel about his experiments and his visitors. Walter had to blink twice before he recognized her as a crotchety Pterodactyl with her wings folded about her like a dressing gown.

"What do you want?" she repeated crossly.

"Um, excuse us, Ma'am," Ralph responded, "but do you know whether Dr. Krebnickel is at home?"

"No, he isn't," she wheezed, her jaws clacking together.

"Do you have any ideas where he might have gone?" Ralph asked gingerly.

Another old Pterodactyl peered around the balcony door. "No we don't," she snapped.

"Do you have any idea when he'll be back?" Walter ventured.

"Unfortunately, I do," snorted the first Pterodactyl. "He mentioned something about the 10:00 bus, so why don't you run along and stop ringing that strange bell of his. Just run along."

The boys mumbled agreement and stumbled down the steps. They could hear the ladies muttering, "Probably blew out every circuit in the house last night with those infernal experiments . . . such noise, such lights . . ."

They walked slowly down the sidewalk. Walter couldn't feel his heart anymore. It was all cold inside his chest. He was depending so much on Dr. Krebnickel's wisdom to know what was wrong. "What are we going to do now?" he asked Ralph.

Ralph put a stubby grey arm around him. "Don't look so sad. It's 9:30 now, so we only have to wait thirty minutes for the bus. There's something I wanted to show you anyway. C'mon!"

Before Walter could reply Ralph dashed across Mars Road into Teehalt Park. Walter ran hesitantly after him, trying to keep all his Dinosaur gear on. The shoes were especially awkward.

As he loped along through a group of kids playing in a sandy spot, something caught his eye and he slowed down. There was a small Triceratops kid bent over some houses and rock gardens he had been building. But Walter was looking at the plastic figures he had all lined up.

"What are those?" he asked.

The kid picked up one of his brightly colored playthings and held it out to Walter. "A Human. I got three whole families."

Walter gulped dismally at the tiny plastic recreations of himself. There were little cars, and dogs and cats, too. But the Humans didn't really look convincing. Their features were too broad and simple.

"Uh, yeah, nice," Walter mumbled.

He continued up the hill as though in a daze, remembering his own toy Dinosaur collection. Ralph had come back to find him and motioned toward Teehalt Branch Library. That must be their destination.

The library was a tall green building with ornate stonework and arched windows. It stood on the corner of Teehalt Park. Inside was cool and dark. The librarian, Mrs. Hunycutt, was a friend of Dr. Krebnickel's. (It was she who had gotten him to donate a lot of his old alchemical scrolls to the library.) Walter liked her. Now she was a lumpy Ankylosaur, an armored Dinosaur.

"Good morning, Ralph and Walter," she said as she stamped a thick leathery volume.

"It's over here," Ralph whispered respectfully as they rounded the desk and entered a dark nook. Then he stood back from a tall glassed exhibit and said, "A Human."

The skeleton stood about nine feet tall. It was blackened with age, but the anatomy was familiar. It was Walter's own, magnified. The plaque on the bottom said it was over a million years old, and was on loan from the Children's Museum. Walter found swallowing hard. He remembered how weird Dinosaur skeletons had seemed to him. Now he was the weird one.

Ralph tugged naggingly at his arm. "There's more, Walter. Come here."

He led Walter to another exhibit, which was well-lighted with morning sun. They brushed past a chubby well-dressed Tyrannosaur sitting by a glass case full of old scrolls. "See," Ralph said enthusiastically, pointing to the pictures in the exhibit, "here's what our world was like millions of years ago when Humans were around."

There were paintings of Humans wallowing through swamps and lounging on the shores of primeval seas. There were photos of sculpted reconstructions with phony plants and painted backdrops. None of the Humans looked very Human to Walter. They looked slightly Saurian, a little too crouchy. But, of course, none of the artists had ever seen a human.

"Neat, huh?" Ralph bubbled.

Suddenly from behind them came a throaty protest. "Librarian!"

The fat Tyrannosaur at the table pointed at the boys as Mrs. Huyncutt lumbered in.

"I do enjoy seeing youngsters respond to the world of science but, alas, their conversation makes it impossible for me to continue my research on DNA amplification." He smiled ingratiatingly at Mrs. Hunycutt. "And perhaps they should learn to observe the library rule of quiet like good citizens."

Mrs. Hunycutt looked troubled. "I didn't hear anything."

"That may be because you are not concentrating on ancient scrolls," the dapper Dinosaur protested.

Walter now saw the Tyrannosaur was reading the Krebnickel Alchemical Archives. One of the yellowed scrolls lay open on the table. Walter couldn't help noticing the title in cramped Old English type: *On Ye Alteration of Ye Animale Syze*.

"I would check this information out if I could, but since I cannot take it, I insist you maintain silence in . . ."

Ralph interrupted the Tyrannosaur's tirade. "Sorry, sorry. We were just going anyway."

Walter gasped in relief and followed Ralph. The last thing he needed was to become the focus of attention. As he passed through a yellow shaft of sunlight he noticed the Tyrannosaur looking closely at him and frowning.

"What's wrong with that boy?" he said sharply, wrinkling up his double chins.

His look chilled Walter. Ralph grabbed him and they both ran outside and down the block.

"Who was that?" Walter shivered. "I thought he suspected something for sure."

Ralph glanced back nervously. "I hope not. That was Dr. Heminglas. You would be in big trouble if he knew you were a Human."

Heminglas! Of course. He would be the only one so interested in Dr. Krebnickel's scrolls. Walter had not recognized him in his Dinosaur version.

"See," said Ralph, pointing to the billboard behind Dr. Krebnickel's distant house. It had a picture of the same Tyrannosaur holding up a bottle and touting,

Buy Heminglas' Patented Wart Enhancer. "Ever since he made a fortune on Dr. Krebnickel's Atomic Wart Formula, he's been trying to steal more secrets."

So, Dr. Heminglas was the same, too. Walter remembered the stories about him—how Dr. Heminglas had known Dr. Krebnickel when they were young in Europe, and how they had worked together until Dr. Heminglas stole Dr. Krebnickel's notebook with all his formulae in it. Heminglas was about the only thing that could get Dr. Krebnickel really mad. Now he had running court battles with him, and was permanently galled by the tacky billboard Heminglas had erected behind Dr. Krebnickel's house. Dr. Heminglas looked even dumber as a Dinosaur, especially a fat one.

Just then the 10:00 bus rolled down Mars Road and wheezed to a stop in front of Dr. Krebnickel's house.

The boys looked at each other hopefully.

"Let's go get this straightened out," Ralph said, "so we don't have to worry about Dr. Heminglas."

3 : *Dr. Krebnickel*

DR. Krebnickel was halfway up the rambling steps to his house when their cries halted him. He turned around and looked through his thick square glasses right over their heads like he always did. Then he looked down and smiled a large smile around his duck bill. Dr. Krebnickel was now a Trachodon, a tall green duckbilled Dinosaur! In place of frizzled white hair around his temples he now had frizzled white scales. But the rumpled, wrinkled baggy clothes were the same, and so was his squeaky accented voice.

"Well, hello, boys. Looking a little pale, aren't you, Walter? Care to step in for some morning tea?"

Just then Walter was distracted by a car moving very, very slowly down Mars Road. It was a slick limousine with a square Saurian front, and as it drove even with the porch, Walter recognized the driver. Dr. Heminglas!

Dr. Krebnickel recognized him, too. He tried to put his bag down, but the books under his arm fell out. Then he fumbled the bag in his other hand and dropped it. He stamped his webbed foot. "What are you doing here? Get out. Go away! No secrets to be stolen today."

Dr. Heminglas only laughed with a gritty sound. He leaned out the car window. "I just wanted to return something your friend dropped at the library, Ladislav," he said through his jeweled cigarette holder, and tossed an object onto the sidewalk. He laughed again as he sped off.

With horror Walter realized the object was his false tail. It must have fallen off in his bustle to leave the library. He ran and retrieved it from the pavement quickly while Ralph calmed Dr. Krebnickel. He hoped no one had noticed his empty tail-sleeve.

"He has no business snooping around here," Dr. Krebnickel muttered. "I've a good mind to climb up and whitewash his sign again."

Dr. Krebnickel was in such a fury that he had to try four lumpy Dinosaur keys before he opened the front door. He was always scatter-brained and forgetful anyway, and anger made him worse.

They carried his things into the cool interior of the house. It was a cavernous old mansion, now even more like a cave. Magazines and books were everywhere, sliding off mounds and stacks of other books. Equations were penciled on door jambs. Notes were stuck all over. Empty doughnut boxes and pickle jars

and potato chip bags were scattered about. Good old Dr. Krebnickel. He was always so busy thinking he didn't seem to mind the clutter.

But if anybody could help Walter, it was Dr. Krebnickel. Although he seemed to be silly and disorganized, Walter had learned that he could get to the root of a mystery, even if he did get there by a roundabout path. But Walter didn't know what he would do when presented with an actual Human child. Would this Dr. Krebnickel react as kindly as his own Dr. Krebnickel? The boys kept looking uneasily at him, afraid to tell him what had happened.

"What a morning!" Dr. Krebnickel exclaimed as he took off his coat. "Rushing downtown for replacement components, having to make do with medium strength titanium chips . . . and of course the new help these days—no help at all. Didn't even know what I was talking about. And when I get back home, that old thief cruising outside!"

Suddenly Walter blurted out, "I'm a Human."

Dr. Krebnickel blinked and said, "Are you sure you feel well, Walter? I could have sworn you said . . ."

"But it's true," Ralph insisted, "he is a Human."

Dr. Krebnickel blinked again and adjusted his glasses, looking through their thick bottoms. "What?"

Then both boys began babbling excitedly about Walter's change. Ralph gestured wildly as he talked; Walter begged for help.

"What's this . . . change? Humans? I'm afraid you'll have to go a little slower, boys."

Walter yanked off the clinging mittens and squeezed out of the football helmet. Dr. Krebnickel's eyes widened. He looked at Walter in amazement as he peeled the clay off his face.

"Why—you're a Human!"

"That's what we've been trying to tell you, Dr. Krebnickel. But I've always been a Human. And so were you the last time I saw you. As a matter of fact, when I went to sleep last night, everybody was a Human. Dinosaurs were extinct!"

The Professaur's bill dropped open and he clapped his hands. "Is it possible . . . can it be?" He produced a large magnifying glass from under a book and looked closely at Walter, muttering, "Amazing . . . simply amazing." The glass made Dr. Krebnickel's awestruck reptile eyes even bigger. They had slit pupils, like a cat's.

"Yes, by Jove!" Dr. Krebnickel exclaimed, slapping his tail to the floor emphatically. "A Human! This is astounding. Revolutionary. Unprecedented. We must get X-rays and measurements as soon as possible."

Dr. Krebnickel turned away as if reaching for some instrument, then looked back at Walter and waddled up close to examine him again. He pulled Walter's arm up and searched its smooth skin, folding his hand and watching it unfurl again.

Walter backed off. "Please don't look at me that way, Dr. Krebnickel. I'm not an exhibit."

"Of course you're not," Dr. Krebnickel said as he released him. "But you certainly would be if other scientists knew about you. You will forgive me, I think, for observing you so closely when you remember you are the only Human I've ever seen . . . amazing! The eye has a circular pupil like the octopus."

"Professaur!" Walter cried.

Dr. Krebnickel stopped looking at him scientifically for a moment. "Tell me, how is it you know me when I have never seen you, Mr. Human?"

Walter threw up his hands. "My name is Walter Fozbek! Yesterday there was a Human Dr. Krebnickel who lived in a house right where this one is. And he was just like you except that he was a Human."

"I see," said Dr. Krebnickel thoughtfully as he leaned back in a great stuffed chair. "And tell me also, umm . . . if you would be so kind, Walter, did my counterpart also have a blue stuffed chair like this?"

"No . . ."

"Aha!"

"He has a brown stuffed chair."

"Oh, hmmmm." The green pebbly skin between Dr. Krebnickel's eyes wrinkled up in thought. "Please, um, Walter, tell me everything that happened this morning. Try to remember all the differences you noticed."

Walter rambled on and on about how things were nearly exactly the same today as yesterday, except that everybody else was a Dinosaur. Ralph testified about

Walter's fright when he first saw him and his confusion at the most ordinary sights.

"And to make matters even worse," Walter added, my parents are coming back tonight to pick me up. They'll be Dinosaurs, and they're sure to notice the change. And Dr. Heminglas knows about me, I think."

"Hmmm," Dr. Krebnickel frowned, "Not good. Fairfax would love to get his claws on a living fossil like you." He focused quickly on Walter. "Oh, no offense intended. But I do see your dilemma."

"That's why we have to find out what's going on," Ralph urged.

Dr. Krebnickel stared blankly into space for a few minutes. Finally he said, "How would you like your tea, boys? Mushrooms and almonds, or sassafras?" Dr. Krebnickel sometimes rambled when he was thinking.

"Sassafras," said Walter, who didn't care anyway. "But what about my problem? What's wrong with me?"

"I don't think it's a matter of you being wrong," Dr. Krebnickel called over his shoulder. "It's just that this is the wrong world for you."

They followed him into his fragrant kitchen where he put tea on to brew.

"What do you mean," Ralph prompted.

"Well," he finally said, "if you really have been Human all along, you must have been Human in a different universe."

"Huh?" said Ralph.

"Wait here," Dr. Krebnickel said, and returned a few minutes later with an old dusty mirror framed with wooden Pteranodon wings. The boys seated themselves wherever they could find an uncluttered perch.

"A universe," Dr. Krebnickel explained, "where Humans are the main species. It must be a mirror of this one, except that there Humans are the rulers and Dinosaurs, such as us, were long gone when the first Human showed up. In other words, in our twin universes, Humans and Dinosaurs are reversed in time, but the universes are so much alike that there is even a Human Ralph and a Human Krebnickel nearly exactly like us."

"Wow," Ralph mused.

Walter whistled thoughtfully. Dr. Krebnickel and Ralph stared at him in a funny way when he did that, for it is impossible to whistle through a Dinosaur beak.

Dr. Krebnickel continued, "There are, no doubt, many worlds matching ours out in the millions of other universes, but they are usually impossible for us to see or reach. They are made of different stuff, you see. Somehow, Walter has switched universes on us."

Since Dr. Krebnickel put it that way, Walter and Ralph had to agree that must have been what happened, but neither of them could guess how.

"That means," Dr. Krebnickel continued, occasionally checking the tea, "that the Walter we know, the Triceratops Walter, must have fallen into the Human world just as this Human Walter was falling into ours, like two people in a revolving door. Right now he is probably talking to the Human Ladislav Krebnickel. Imagine that—the Human me must even now be explaining these things to our lost Walter. But that leaves the large matter of how you came to transfer worlds. And how to get you back, of course. Come along then, let us see which Dr. Krebnickel will crack the riddle first!''

4 : *Quarwyn*

DR. Krebnickel led them down the carpeted steps to his cellar laboratory, his tail thumping down each one after him. Walter was careful not to step on it. The door had a giant bolt and a combination lock, which Dr. Krebnickel managed to open after three tries.

The lab was vast. Lighted panels all around the ceiling made it seem bright as day without dazzling. All the Doctor's equipment lay gleaming on cabinets and tables, books to the roof in heavy oak cases, bottles and vials in brick cubbies all around the room. There were old machines everywhere, rewired by Dr. Krebnickel to serve his purposes. An old washing machine was now a centrifuge and an ancient sewing machine doubled as part of an electron microscope. A huge electronic computer like a maze of quartz crystals stood at the other end of the room.

In the center, surrounded by desks and shelves was a tremendous curtain suspended by hooks from the ceiling. Behind the curtain lay the Professaur's Top Secret power source, the Neutrino Turbine, hidden from Dr. Heminglas' spying. The ceiling was blackened by circuitry blowouts. And from the freshness of the burns, recent blowouts.

Dr. Krebnickel went around turning things on and clearing places for them to sit. Walter looked expectantly at all of the equipment. He sure hoped the answer to his problem was here.

Dr. Krebnickel returned and admired Walter. He had him stand behind a screen that showed all his bones. "Amazing! Marvelous! None of the skeletons we have recovered have been this complete."

"Of course not," Walter scowled. "Mine's inside me. Look, Dr. Krebnickel, I know you must be curious, but when are you going to find out what made me change?"

Dr. Krebnickel looked at him blankly for a second. "Oh, yes. Of course. Forgive me. It's just that . . . I simply *must* take some X-rays of you before you return. This is too huge an opportunity, besides, you could always pop away to your own world the way you came, and here I would be without any evidence."

Walter whimpered, "Find out how to return me, and you can take any kind of picture you want!"

"Hold . . . that . . . pose," Dr. Krebnickel whispered, then pressed a bulb leading to the machine.

Clicks and whirs followed. "Got it! A perfect Human skeleton on film."

Walter sighed. It was no use trying to stop the Professaur when he was in a scientific frenzy.

"Now, where were we?" Dr. Krebnickel looked blankly into space.

"Getting Walter back," Ralph coaxed.

"Yes, of course," Dr. Krebnickel said. "A very complicated problem. I really wish I could call Quarwyn into play. I will need all the brainpower at my disposal. Unfortunately, that is impossible."

Quarwyn was the name of Dr. Krebnickel's special computer. It had crystalline circuits and was rooted deep in the earth beneath the house. Dr. Krebnickel said it knew things he didn't even know how to ask about.

"Why?" Walter said.

Dr. Krebnickel nibbled worrisomely at a thick claw. "Oh," he said, glancing uneasily at the end of the room where Quarwyn slept, "I kept him up until all hours last night. We . . . we had to do a lot of computing. Then some of the equipment blew, you see, and I kept him up to make repairs. Frightfully exhausting."

"But this is an emergency," Ralph protested. "Walter's parents are coming to get him and we have to get him back!"

"Oh, yes, yes," Dr. Krebnickel gestured nervously. "But you've never seen Quarwyn angry. He can be very nasty, even violent."

"Oh yeah," Walter said. "Well, has he ever seen a really mad Human kid run amuck?"

"Please," Dr. Krebnickel begged, "there is no need for strong emotions. If he hears you . . ."

"Quarwyyyyyyyyyyyn!" Walter shrieked.

"No, no," Dr. Krebnickel's hands fluttered frantically. "He'll be angry—I'll never hear the end of it—"

"Quarwyn, wake up!" Walter thundered.

He hopped off his seat and ran to where Quarwyn stood like a sleeping mineral cathedral, Dr. Krebnickel bounding after. Just as he was about to shriek again the Professaur grabbed him from behind, stifling him with one thorny green hand.

Dr. Krebnickel swung him around and whispered fiercely, "Ssshhhhhhhhh! You'll wake him up!"

Walter gave him a dumb look. "Wake who up?"

"Quarwyn!" Dr. Krebnickel hollered, losing his temper.

Quarwyn woke up.

"Violence!" Quarwyn thundered in his odd crystal voice. "Villainy! Who dares disturb Quarwyn's slumber?" Test tubes rattled in their racks and the glow from the computer's lights bathed the whole room in phosphorescence. Sparks crackled between crystals.

Dr. Krebnickel cringed, trying to sink beneath the table. "We did, um . . ."

"WHAT? SPEAK UP?!"

"We did, Quarwyn," Dr. Krebnickel said some-

what louder. "I know I promised to let you sleep but we have a terribly difficult problem, and as long as you're up, could you help us? Ralph and Walter are here."

A rumble shook the laboratory. "Help you, indeed!"

"Now wait a minute, you feisty old silicon forest!" Dr. Krebnickel suddenly snapped. "These boys need just fifteen minutes of your time to get out of a terrible fix. I'm not asking for myself."

There was a long spell of icy silence from the wall of quartz. Finally there was a sound like chimes sighing in the wind, and Quarwyn said, "Oh, very well. What is the urgent problem this time?"

Briefly Dr. Krebnickel repeated their story.

"Ahhh," said Quarwyn, his sensors examining Walter. "Yes. I haven't seen one of those for ages. At least a million circuits of the sun. Yes. I detect abnormalities in the creature's electromagnetic field. It smells of warpage."

"W-warpage?" Walter croaked.

"Affirmed," the computer replied. "A warp in space. A crimp in time. You folded the universe."

"I didn't mean to," Walter sniffed.

"Of course you didn't," Dr. Krebnickel comforted. "Just what are you saying, Quarwyn?"

"As you suspected, Doctor, this Walter is from a different universe. His is a mirror image of ours. The two Walters switched universes."

"A double disappearance," Dr. Krebnickel muttered.

"But how?" Ralph asked confusedly.

Quarwyn's lights blinked and sputtered. "Were I to venture a guess, I would say a certain dimensional singularity was involved . . ."

"Oh, dear," Dr. Krebnickel gulped.

". . . acting on a peculiar flux in the wavelength of a chemical element."

"What?" Dr. Krebnickel quizzed. "But which element do you think we are dealing with?"

"Smells like Xenon to me," said Quarwyn casually.

"But what about . . ." Dr. Krebnickel began.

"Enough, Professaur. Use your own brain for a change, pitiful as it is. Mine needs a rest. Good night."

"But Quarwyn . . ."

"Go away!"

Quarwyn's circuits dimmed. Dr. Krebnickel threw up his hands in exasperation.

"What's a dim . . . dimensional singularity?" Ralph asked.

"And what has it got to do with me?" Walter added desperately.

"Have you ever heard of a Black Hole?" Dr. Krebnickel sighed.

5: *The Black Hole*

"I was running some routine experiments yesterday afternoon, when my Neutrino Turbine blew out. Quarwyn and I worked until about midnight repairing it."

Dr. Krebnickel looked at the confusion in their faces. "Wait a moment and I will show you what I am talking about."

The Professaur dug around in a box of junk beside the turbine until he located a bizarre brass helmet and stuffed his head into it. Then he disappeared behind the curtains with lights blinking all over his helmet. A long period of silence followed.

When he emerged he was holding an old pickle jar with the label partially scraped off. There was a spiral wire taped around it connected to a whirring box on top. He sat down on a bench and removed the helmet.

Walter looked closely. It was awful dark inside

the jar. It was so black it was purple. Walter felt queasy.

"This jar contains a very special object which I obtained at great peril and expense. Its function is far too complicated for even me to understand, so I won't confuse you with that. But it is vital to the turbine. It contains a tiny Black Hole."

Ralph's eyes got super wide. "You mean a space warp?"

"Roughly speaking, yes. It has the strongest gravity of any object in the known universe so it sucks space in around itself like a vacuum cleaner. I captured it one night near Andromeda. Put up a devil of a fight."

"But how can it be in that jar without sucking the whole earth in after it?" Walter gulped.

"Oh, no danger, no danger at all when you know how to trap them and set up the right electromagnetic field around them. This particular one is troublesome though. Every couple of days—I haven't discovered the pattern yet—it simply goes out. Or goes somewhere else. However, with this helmet on, I can descend into the jar, reclaim it, and return safely." He paused. "The Black Hole escaped yesterday afternoon. It was midnight by the time Quarwyn and I got it back."

Walter looked at the jar with awe. "Then you think that when that thing escaped yesterday . . ."

"Yes, it may have had something to do with your transfer, but not by itself."

Walter looked at him blankly.

"You see," Dr. Krebnickel continued, "if it were only the Black Hole that caused your transfer, you would have disappeared yesterday afternoon—when the Hole escaped—instead of during the night. There must be another element in your change. Quarwyn says it's Xenon, the rare gas, but I can't imagine how." Dr. Krebnickel set the helmet down. "If only I still had my Xenon spectacles!" he muttered.

"But if that's a hole," Ralph asked, "where is the other end?"

Dr. Krebnickel shrugged. "No one knows."

"But Professaur," Walter exclaimed as he bounded up, "don't you see? My world is at the other end of the hole! All you have to do is let me wear that helmet and go through the hole and I'll be back home."

Dr. Krebnickel held up one hand, chuckling. "Wouldn't work, I assure you. Xenon is involved somehow with something you were doing when the hole escaped. Otherwise, dozens of people would have awakened as Humans. Ralph here, for example."

Walter sat back, deflated.

"Think back, Walter," Dr. Krebnickel suggested. "Was there anything special you were doing yesterday about 3 o'clock? Anything at all that might help us?"

Walter thought and thought. He shook his head. "We were just playing in the park. Nothing unusual."

"Perhaps if I took a blood sample it might give us a clue . . ." Dr. Krebnickel suggested.

"You sure you won't let me try to go through the Black Hole?"

Dr. Krebnickel shook his head emphatically. "Too dangerous, and it wouldn't work, besides."

"Well," said Ralph, winking at Walter, "how do *you* go into it?"

"Oh, I merely put on the H32 helmet and turn the dial on the side to the same number as on the dial on the jar. And the Black Hole sucks me into the bottle. When I want to return I simply turn the dial back to zero and close my eyes."

"Sometimes you're weird, Doc," said Ralph.

"Oh, not me. Reality is far stranger than myself. You can't even imagine how very odd things are, to the core. But now that Quarwyn won't help us, I shall have to get out my blood analysis unit and look for Xenon in Walter's blood."

"Couldn't we have some tea first?" Ralph asked slyly.

"Why, surely. The tea! Give me time to rethink the problem as well. We may be starting at the wrong end, you know . . ."

Dr. Krebnickel disappeared up the stairs muttering to himself about DNA and enzymes. Walter looked at Ralph.

"What is all this winking about? And the tea? You hate Dr. Krebnickel's tea."

"Sssshh!" whispered Ralph. He was hoisting the H32 helmet up to the table beside Walter. "Now we can get you to your own universe before supper."

"How? What are you talking about?"

"Seventeen-oh-one," Ralph read from the dial on top of the Black Hole jar. "I'm talking about you going into the Black Hole and back to your own world." He set the helmet dial carefully.

"Wait a minute! I don't know how to travel through a Black Hole."

"Well, then, you'll just have to stay here tonight and see your parents and hope the Professaur can solve your problem," Ralph said sternly. "Unless Dr. Heminglas captures you first, that is."

"Oh," said Walter.

"Well, make up your mind. Here comes the Professaur with the tea! Either turn the helmet on and try the Black Hole now or take your chances. It's your decision."

Walter fingered the switch on the side of the helmet. He could hear Dr. Krebnickel humming as he neared the stairs. Walter decided.

Dr. Krebnickel came down the steps with a tray full of teacups and a steaming kettle.

"Where's Walter?" he said.

6 : *The Barrier*

ZZZZZZZIIIIIIIIIIIINNNNNNNNNNGGGGG!!,   the
universe turned into the sound of a giant angry bee the
second Walter pushed the switch.

SSSSSSSWWWWOOOOOOOOOOOOOOOOOOOOOOPPPPPP!

He flew through empty darkness. He couldn't see a thing. He felt as if he were being squeezed super tiny and stretched super large at the same time. He couldn't catch his breath, like when you have the wind knocked out of you or go on a million-mile-an-hour roller coaster. He tried, but couldn't make any noises. He thought he was going to die.

POP!

Suddenly he could breathe again. When he opened his eyes he found himself floating weightlessly in dark space. In the distance a lavender light glowed dully in the gloom. He felt himself spinning slowly toward it.

From beyond the light, a shadow seemed to be floating with him. He could see through the dim lavender glow enough to tell there was something there, something whose arms and legs were moving as slowly as his.

Walter righted himself and tried to run. His legs pulled along thickly, then, with each step, they grew lighter. His running became more normal as the light grew until . . .

Wham!

Walter was knocked flat by a strange clear barrier with facets cut in it like a gem. He shook his head and got up. Before him was a smooth lavender wall. The shadow on the other side was still there, obviously just beyond its surface. He could see a dim hand touching it just as his was, but he could make out no details.

Walter tried to communicate with it by tapping on

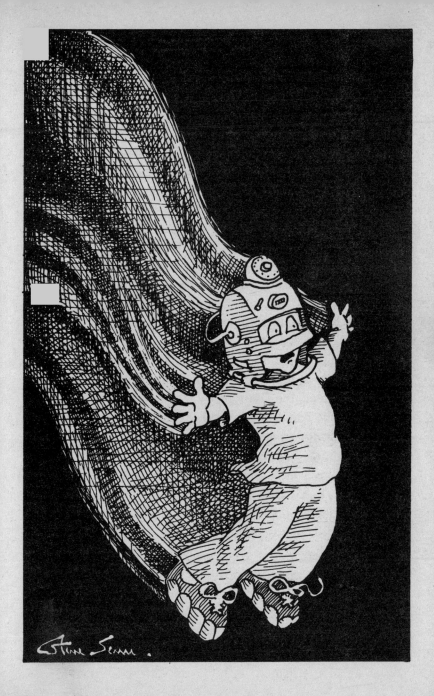

the smooth barrier. It apparently had the same idea, for the figure was thumping, too. But it was no use—Walter didn't even know Morse Code.

Then he remembered the crayons Ralph had stuffed in the top pocket of his Dinosaur shirt. In a flash Walter whipped an orange one out, and began lettering carefully on the lavender pane.

?UOY ERA OHW, he wrote. The letters glowed in the violet air. Walter didn't know how he expected his counterpart to reply, but he had to try.

Walter's jaw dropped in astonishment when he saw identical orange letters slowly crawling across the other side of the glass. Hesitantly, whoever was writing was struggling to letter backwards also. NAME WALTER FOZBEK, it said.

"But . . . but . . ." Walter sputtered to himself. Then a flood of realization hit him. It was the other Walter, the Dinosaur Walter Fozbek on the other side of the barrier, searching for the way back into his own world! Walter nearly dropped his crayon in excitement as he lettered back, !OOT EMAN YM.

There was a long pause, then the other crayon replied, YOU'RE ME?

Walter nodded as he wrote, !NAMUH.

WEIRD, was the reply.

?EREH FO TUO TEG EW OD WOH, Walter wrote.

LOOKS LIKE WE'RE BLOCKED, came the disappointing response. Then the moving orange letters wrote slowly on, BUT HAVE YOU SEEN WHERE THE LIGHT IS COMING FROM?

Light? He must mean the violet glow. Walter hadn't noticed. He looked about him in the blackness, then saw the other crayon was drawing an arrow upward. His gaze followed the arrow over his head.

There, radiating in a purple glow as they hung embedded in the barrier, were a pair of glasses. Glasses with faceted sides and strange little boxes on the corners. Walter had a nagging feeling in the back of his mind—where had he seen them before? Of course! Now he remembered!

He reached up . . . but they were a little too high. His jump was a dismal failure, for he only moved a fraction upward. The gravity in this place was too thick. He put everything he had into it . . . and pushed upward against the force, nearly touching the edge of the glasses. He fell back with the weight of a thousand Walters. He could feel his molecules compressing as he slammed down.

Walter clenched his fists. Anger surged into him. For the first time today he felt he could fight back. He scrunched down, wiggling the Triceratopsian sneakers to get traction, and set his eyes on those glasses. He took a collossal leap, kicking with all the anger in him. As slow as sunrise his fingertips rose through the darkness closer . . . closer. He had them! His hand closed over the glasses and he pulled. Gravity did the rest. The glasses slid from the grip of the clear wall with a pop and tumbled back down with him.

He slipped the glasses on nervously. Everything was fuzzy for a second, then things cleared. Instead of a vague image on the other side of the barrier he now saw the other Walter Fozbek fitting his own glasses on. He was a Triceratops wearing a bronze H32 helmet. Walter waved. The kid grinned and waved back.

?SESSALG EHT REBMEMER, he wrote in a clear place on the wall.

The other Walter nodded and wrote back, YES, BUT HOW DID THEY GET HERE?

Walter shook his head. WONK LLIW LEKCIN-BERK .RD EBYAM, he wrote hopefully.

YES, the other Walter replied, LET'S GO BACK AND ASK HIM.

KCUL DOOG, Walter wrote finally.

He stepped back from the faceted barrier and watched the other Walter wave and turn his dial back to zero. There was a flash of green light and he was gone. Walter hesitated a moment with his hand on his dial. It isn't every day that you get to see yourself from another world. He didn't make a bad looking Dinosaur.

He sighed, shut his eyes and turned the dial to zero.

7 : *The Riddle of Return*

BBBBZZZZZIIIIIIIIIINNNNGGGG!

The cold black velvet roller coaster took him again on its million mile an hour ride back from the Black Hole. Then he began vibrating rapidly.

POP! He was lying face down on the floor of the laboratory. Above him he heard Ralph's excited voice, "You went to a Black Hole, Walter! What was it like?"

"Are you all right, my boy?" Dr. Krebnickel sounded concerned.

Walter dragged himself to his feet and turned around. Dr. Krebnickel was looking at him in an odd way. As a matter of fact, there were several Dr. Krebnickels, and they were lavender. He was still wearing the strange glasses!

"Look, Doc," he nearly shouted, snatching them off. "Look what I found!"

Dr. Krebnickel took them gently, as if they were a precious treasure, and he still looked at them strangely. "Do you know where these spectacles came from, Walter?" he said slowly.

"Yeah," Walter beamed, "I finally remembered what I did unusual yesterday—I found those glasses."

"Huh?" Ralph grunted. "I thought you found them in the Hole."

"There too," Walter began to explain, as Ralph helped him out of the H32 helmet. His hair was all sweaty and stuck to his head. The Professaur handed him a steaming cup of tea and shoved a crate over for him to sit on. Walter sagged onto it and gulped down some of the brew.

"Do you know what those are?" Dr. Krebnickel fairly bubbled. "My spectacles, my electromagnetic Xenon spectacles, that vanished mysteriously two years ago."

Walter quirked one eyebrow. "I don't know anything about that. All I know is I found them in a squirrel nest in one of the trees in Teehalt Park. Then there they were, in the Black Hole."

"Squirrels! Drat! I must remember to keep those windows closed. Amazing. These must be the missing element of your transfer, then. Xenon. Quarwyn was right!"

Walter grinned, proud of himself.

"What's going on?" Ralph whined miserably.

Walter laughed. "Well, as near as I can figure, I found the glasses yesterday in the park. I remember trying them on, and then feeling all queasy and the world seeming to spin. Then there was a rushing in my ears, and the glasses popped off and I couldn't find them. I forgot about it until they showed up in the Black Hole . . .''

"Eureka!" Dr. Krebnickel suddenly shouted. "The spectacles must have reacted with the Black Hole and opened up the doorway between worlds for you. The Hole sucked the glasses up into it as it left the laboratory . . ."

"Then, during the night," Walter finished. "Dr. Krebnickel recaptured the Black Hole, and I fell through the doorway into this world."

"Exactly!" the Professaur triumphed.

Slowly comprehension dawned on Ralph. "You mean Walter found your lost glasses at the same time the Black Hole escaped, and that's what pulled him through?"

Dr. Krebnickel nodded so hard his glasses nearly fell off. "The final transfer happened when I trapped the Black Hole last night and imprisoned it. The gravitational pull must have done it. Walter swapped worlds while he was sleeping."

"Yeah," Walter said.

"I love a mystery solved," Dr. Krebnickel said smugly, turning the Xenon spectacles slowly in the light.

"But . . ." Walter said, with a shiver, "what do we do to get me back?"

Dr. Krebnickel's face went blank.

"Yeah," Ralph said. "Going through the Black Hole didn't work. And Walter found the glasses and that didn't change anything. All we know is how the transfer happened."

"Wait a minute!" Dr. Krebnickel squealed. "Let me think a moment. There must be a way . . . wait!"

He dropped his teacup and rushed to a strange sort of computer made of an old adding machine and a color TV tube. As he typed in figures, he kept shaking his head and mumbling to himself.

Walter's hopes sank. Dr. Krebnickel still didn't have the answer. Ralph was right, he should already be home.

"I'm stuck!" he wailed. "I'm a Human kid trapped in a world of Dinosaurs. I'll never get home again. I'll grow up in a museum!"

Dr. Krebnickel wrung his green hands helplessly. "Please . . . I should be able to work this out soon. If I take the wavelength of the Xenon divided by a factor of a million . . . I may be able to find the answer in a few days," he paused, "or weeks."

"Oh, no," Ralph moaned. "We can't wait."

Walter looked at Ralph and then they both looked at the silent bank of crystals that was Quarwyn. Dr. Krebnickel followed their gaze and swallowed heavily.

"No . . . we can't," he stammered. "I don't know what he'll do if I wake him up again."

"We've got to ask him how to get Walter back!" Ralph said.

"WAKE UP!" Walter yelled through cupped hands.

"Sssssshhhhh!" Dr. Krebnickel waved frantically, then tried to cover the computer's sensors.

"HELP!" Ralph chimed. "Daaaaaarwin, wake up."

"Not Darwin," Dr. Krebnickel snapped, "Quarwyn!"

BAM! The room blazed into light. Sparks flew from an antenna on Quarwyn and zapped the end of the Professaur's tail. He yelped and dove behind a cabinet. The boys scrambled. Quarwyn's circuits glowed cherry-red with anger.

"*OUTRAGE!*" Quarwyn bellowed. "*Again* you dare bring me back from peaceful mineral dreams!"

Dr. Krebnickel just whimpered behind the cabinet.

There was something like a groan from the computer. "All right! All right. I can't stand to see a grown Trachodon cry. What's the problem now?"

Briefly Walter explained what had happened from behind the safety of a crate.

"So. The Human found the Xenon spectacles," Quarwyn sighed. "By accident. Brilliant. He discovered that he couldn't get through the Black Hole because of the Xenon barrier. And now he wants to know how to transfer back?" There was a silence. "Young creature, don't you recall anything else about what you did while wearing the glasses?"

Walter shook his head.

Quarwyn's lights raced in patterns as he scanned Walter. Finally he said, "It's quite simple."

Dr. Krebnickel peeked around the cabinet curiously.

"BUT," Quarwyn barked, "because my sleep has been disturbed, I will not give you the answer directly."

Walter moaned. "But . . ."

"Instead, you get to use *your* brains for a change. Don't overload your circuits, Professaur. GOOD NIGHT!"

The thunder and lightning faded. A bell rang as a strip of paper slipped from a slot in Quarwyn's side. Dr. Krebnickel gingerly tore it off and examined it.

"Drat the machine," he hissed. "It has its silly revenge. It's a riddle!"

Walter snatched the paper away and the boys read:

> You'll have to think to find the link,
> 'Twixt reptiles alive and ones extinct,
>
> A cousin of those that didn't endure,
> With family resemblance in miniature,
>
> A hopper, a flopper, a born camouflager,
> Garden dweller and treetop lodger,
>
> To fixup this mixup a roundup must be,
> Of a forgotten branch of Zoology.

"What?" Ralph shrilled. "Who could guess that!"

"Calmly," Dr. Krebnickel licked his lips nervously. "There's an answer there somewhere. Think. The link between . . . family resemblance . . . a hopper and flopper. Does that ring any bells, Walter?"

Walter's mind raced desperately, jumping from word to word of the puzzle. This wasn't fair!

"A cousin of those that didn't endure?" Ralph pondered. "Wouldn't that be a monkey?"

"Perhaps," Dr. Krebnickel said, "unless Quarwyn means the extinct Dinosaurs on Walter's home planet . . ."

Walter thought. Sweat popped out on his clay-smeared brow.

"To fixup this mixup a roundup must be . . ." Ralph read. "Does that mean what we're looking for is round?"

Walter's heart sagged. It was impossible. He felt hopelessness begin to overtake him.

"Hmmmmm," Dr. Krebnickel mused scratching his chin, "a forgotten branch of Zoology . . ."

Walter's eyes flashed open and he whooped. "A forgotten branch! That's it!"

"That's what?" Ralph said impatiently.

"A lizard! I had forgotten that too! When I tried on your glasses yesterday up in that tree, there was a little green lizard with a broken tail and a dark spot on a branch . . . the forgotten branch! I tried looking at him through the glasses, and that's when I got dizzy."

"That's it!" Dr. Krebnickel shouted, smacking his forehead in sudden understanding. "It is all explained!"

Ralph wore a disgusted frown. "Will someone please tell me what a lizard has to do with all this?"

"The lizard was Walter's doorway," Dr. Krebnickel smiled contentedly. "Human Walter here found Human Krebnickel's glasses at the same time our Dinosaur Walter found mine. They both tried them on, and looked at a lizard at the same time the Black Hole escaped."

"I know all that," Ralph was getting annoyed. "But what does the lizard have to do with it?"

"The lizard is the link between the living and extinct species of both worlds." Dr. Krebnickel went on, ignoring Ralph's tone. "Here, it is our cousin, there it is a descendent of their Dinosaurs. The gravity of the Black Hole twisted the glasses, mixing up Walter's ancestry. The lizard was the hinge that the doorway opened on."

Ralph's beak fell open. "Like Alice through the looking glass," He said in awe.

"Well, that explains it," said Walter without cheer, "but it doesn't get me back to my world."

"Yeah," said Ralph, "How do we get Walter *back* through the mirror?"

"Elementary," smiled Dr. Krebnickel. "We must merely get the lizard that Walter looked at and get him to look through the glasses at it once more. Then everything will be restored. That must be what Quarwyn meant! To fixup this mixup, we round up all the lizards in the park."

"But only Walter knows the right lizard," Ralph

WALTER FOUND DR. KREBNICKEL'S
XENON  SPECTACLES
AND LOOKED AT A LIZARD...

AND FELL INTO A DINOSAUR WORLD
BECAUSE...

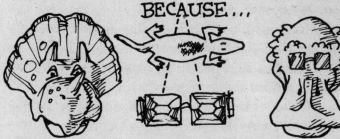

DINOSAUR WALTER FOUND DR. KREBNICKEL'S
XENON SPECTACLES
AND LOOKED AT THE MATCHING LIZARD
IN THE DINOSAUR WORLD THROUGH THEM,
SWAPPING PLACES.

protested. "Lots of lizards have broken tails and spots!"

"That's why we must catch them all, to make sure we get the right one. Since our two universes are mirror images, the lizard we want should look the same. We had better catch them all and let Walter examine them all."

"Do you know how many lizards are in Teehalt Park?" Walter howled.

"Several dozen I should think," said Dr. Krebnickel. "Ours should be a bit adventurous to be on a lower limb, so hopefully we won't have to climb any trees. Still, we'd better get started catching them as soon as possible. I have some old butterfly nets upstairs."

While Dr. Krebnickel bumped upstairs to find the nets, Ralph replaced Walter's Triceratops helmet, despite his grumbling. If he was going outside, he would have to look like a Dinosaur. If anyone saw that he was a Human there would be panic in the park, and Walter dreaded the thought of what could happen to him. Besides, Dr. Heminglas still might be lurking around. Walter shivered. Ralph smoothed out all the modelling clay and made Walter put the mittens on again.

"I'll call mom," Ralph said thoughtfully, "and tell her we will be eating lunch over here so she won't miss us."

By the time the phone call had been made nets had been found for each of them, and Dr. Krebnickel brought out a soft drink carton loaded with empty pickle jars for the lizards.

"All the lizards?" Walter asked.

"Every one," Dr. Krebnickel replied.

And so they descended from Dr. Krebnickel's house and into the depths of Teehalt Park.

8 : *The Search*

"RALPH, you take the area from the baseball diamond up to the library. Walter, you catch all the lizards in the main part of the park where the trees are. I'll take the playground and the brook. Each take a bottle with you and return for another when that is full. When we have finished, we shall all three scour the library, where no doubt the remaining lizards will have fled. Is that clear?"

Ralph and Walter nodded.

Then they went to their separate areas, cautiously examining shrubs and trees. Walter's part of the park was a wide rolling grassy plain presided over by groves of tall oak trees.

The scene was much as it might be on his world. There was a family picnic going on up the slope. The mother Corythosaur had spread a circular blanket for her husband and a couple of chubby kids. One of the kids was toddling around in grey diapers swung under its tail. Walter noticed a stroller next to them on the grass with a huge spotted egg in it sunning.

There were a couple of teenage Dimetrodons playing frisbee in the shadows. They honked occasionally in glee as one or the other missed. Then, as Walter watched, a third Dinosaur joined the game. A young Pteranodon wearing a red T-shirt swooped through the branches and snatched the frisbee in mid-flight.

He sighed. He would have some strange memories to take back with him, if he ever got back. He began scanning tree trunks.

He caught his first lizard on an oak trunk. It scurried away from him quickly, but he got it. Catching it made his heart pound. Into the bottle with it. It was a small one, and its tail was pretty straight for a lizard. Not really like the one he'd seen through the Xenon spectacles, but they had to catch them all to make sure. He chased another through the grass right between the frisbee players.

"Hey, whatcha doin'?" one of them said.

"Catching lizards," Walter confessed hesitantly.

"Why?" The frisbee game had stopped, and all three players were watching him.

"Uh, for a science project," Walter gulped.

"Hey, look!" honked the sharp-eyed Pteranodon, "he's wearing mittens."

"Whatcha wearin' gloves in July for, kid?"

Walter nervously slipped the captive lizard into the jar while backing off, he hoped nonchalantly. "Oh, 'cause I'm allergic to grass," he mumbled. "My mom makes me wear them."

The Pteranodon's beady eyes flashed over him suspiciously. "You look kind of weird, kid."

Walter scooped up the frisbee and tossed it high into the air. "Catch!" he shouted, turned, and ran away as fast as he could. When he turned around, the players had resumed their game. Walter let out a long anxious breath.

In the next forty-five minutes Walter managed to find four more lizards, and catch three of them. The other one escaped to the rocks around the brook and he decided that was Dr. Krebnickel's territory. After he caught his fifth lizard, Walter relaxed against a big oak tree. It was hot underneath the football helmet. His Dinosaur gloves were awfully uncomfortable.

All of a sudden he felt very lonely. He felt like he might have to wear a disguise the rest of his life to live in this world. Or worse, become a famous natural wonder. He could see the circus advertisements: AMAZING! STUPENDOUS! SEE THE LIVE HUMAN BOY! He didn't want to be a carnival exhibit on this reptile planet. He wanted to be someplace where he could just be himself. Plain Walter Fozbek. It made him miss his parents. Even his dumb little brother. He had never known how happy he was with them.

There was a lizard perched on his shoe blinking

at him. Walter eased his net above it and then quickly snared the lizard and his shoe. He held the wriggling lizard up in the net. Well, the only way he was going to get back to his own space was to catch as many lizards as he could and hope that they could find the right one. He juggled the lizard into position and snapped it quickly into the jar before the other lizards could escape.

After he had taken that jar back and gotten an empty, he worked on the oak trees at the far corner of the park, where a bridge ran over the brook. He caught two unsuspecting lizards sunning themselves on a bench. It only took one swoop to net them both. Into the bottle. He had to hang upside-down over the bridge railing to capture one hiding in a crack between two stones. Just as he managed to get his net around it, he heard a voice. "Young saur, what are you doing with these lizards?" He righted himself to find three dowdy Stegosaur ladies on bicycles looking at him disapprovingly, their spines bristling. Uneasily, he jailed his last lizard.

"Uh, we're collecting specimens from Teehalt Park."

"And who might 'we' be?" said one of the ladies.

"Me, and Ralph, and Dr. Krebnickel."

"Dr. Krebnickel!" The ladies exchanged glances. "We should have known. That old Trachodon should be committed. What do you intend to do with all this wildlife?"

"We're just going to run some tests. Just take some readings. We won't hurt them," Walter said as he edged awkwardly away from the Stegosaurs.

Their tiny pointed faces looked indignant. "But by taking these creatures from their natural environment who knows what kind of damage you will be doing the park's ecology? They are our cousins, you know."

Walter began to perspire. If they knew what he had really done to the ecology of their whole planet, he was sure they would have rendered him extinct right there to match the rest of the Humans. "We're only borrowing them for a couple of hours," he said. "Then we're going to let them all go."

"That's not the point. You ought not to be meddling with natural things. We must notify the Friends of the Trees Society immediately. Come, Cora."

And the three ladies pedaled off furiously down the street. Walter overheard Cora say something about "that peculiar looking child." He straightened his helmet.

Walter moaned. He was all for protecting the environment. But the Friends of the Trees were crazy. They would Super-Glue all the aerosol cans in the drugstore shut so they couldn't pollute, or they would surprise people burning autumn leaves and dowse them and the leaves with water. And they protected a lot of animals who could take care of themselves. Like the April Wharf Rat Drive they had held. And the Save Our Cockroaches Day. Sometimes they were

right, but usually their methods turned everybody off. Walter sure hoped the old ladies were just talking. All he needed was a bunch of Tree-freaks to cause a commotion.

He ran down the sloping lawn toward Ralph, who was peering into the shrubs around Teehalt Library. The sun was high overhead. As he ran, Walter caught sight of Dr. Krebnickel's net flashing up over the banks of the brook.

He felt a little better. Even if they were Dinosaurs, Walter still had friends. Friends are friends, no matter what else they are.

"Your head is on crooked," Ralph said to Walter as he ran up.

"I can't help it. The straps are loose. They were made for a Dinosaur chin." Walter adjusted his face again. "We may have some trouble soon. I ran into some Friends of the Trees, and they didn't like what I was doing with the lizards."

"Uh-oh. I hope we're finished before they decide to come back and picket us. I don't think your disguise could stand too much close examination. Let's just take a last look around before we go," Ralph said.

Ralph covered the back of the shrubs while Walter poked around in them with his net. Suddenly, a fat green lizard zipped between his legs and sped up the wall of the library.

"Ooops," Walter said.

Ralph cursed. "I've been trying to get that one for fifteen minutes!"

The lizard sat on top of an air conditioner winking at them. It was infuriating.

Walter made a swipe at it, but it was a fast little devil. It hopped onto the window. It was too high to reach so Walter grabbed the adjacent air conditioner with one hand and jumped onto the ledge at the bottom of the building. There was just enough room to stand on. He poised himself and carefully snapped the net around the lizard. It made a loud whack on the pane, but he got the lizard. Now to get it in a bottle. Ralph climbed up on the other side and leaned over to poke the bottle under the net. Suddenly he was poking into a curious face behind the net.

It was Mrs. Hunycutt, the librarian, looking at them. Walter snapped the net back. The lizard blinked maliciously, and suddenly Walter realized it had a big brown splotch on its back and a broken tail. It looked like the Xenon doorway lizard, but he wasn't sure.

Just then Mrs. Hunycutt slid the window up to speak. The lizard slid up and out of reach on the window pane, then bounded up the wall.

"What's up, Ralph?" Mrs. Hunycutt asked casually.

Ralph's shoulders sagged. "Our lizard is, now. We were trying to catch it. It's gone."

She smiled a friendly Ankylosaur smile. "You shouldn't have much trouble finding another one.

Please don't climb on the library building, though. It's not safe, and if you got hurt . . ."

"It would be the library's fault," Walter said.

"That's right. Gotta go now. Have fun." Mrs. Hunycutt slid the window down and waved them an armored farewell.

9 : *Panic in the Park*

THEY walked glumly away from the library. By this time Dr. Krebnickel was through with the brook. He was coming toward them with the bottle rack rattling beside him.

"How have we done, my young friends?" he said, setting down the rack.

They handed him their bottles and told him about the escaped lizard, the Friends of the Trees, and Mrs. Hunycutt.

"Well, we appear to have captured ummm . . . exactly 28 of our fellow reptiles (excuse me, Walter). Very good job, boys. But I still think we must have a thorough search of the library grounds before we conclude our outing and retire to the laboratory. Mrs. Hunycutt will pose no problem. We simply must be circumspect about it. Arouse no undue attention, you know."

"What about him?" said Walter, thumbing at the big green lizard sitting high on the back wall. "I hate to let him get away because he looks kind of like the Xenon lizard."

Dr. Krebnickel sighed. "I'll get him. You boys check the other side."

Walter walked around with Ralph to the front of the building. There was a wide row of steps climbing to the door. Walter casually inspected the left side of the building while Ralph walked around nonchalantly on the right. There was a tiny baby lizard on the sill of a high window. Walter got it with a minimum of scrambling. He was pretty good at catching lizards by now. But it did make the Dinosaurs entering the library stare to see the two of them with nets and bottles.

"Got one? Good." Ralph said.

Walter nodded and stepped around the corner of the building. There were no lizards, but he could feel Mrs. Hunycutt looking at him. She tapped on the window to get his attention but he pretended not to hear her. He came back to the back of the library to see Ralph and Dr. Krebnickel standing together looking at the wall. Ralph had not found any more lizards either. And the big green lizard was still further from the ground. He was now on the fancy sculpted frieze that ran around the building.

"Well, boys," said Dr. Krebnickel, "We simply must get to the roof. I shall have to have a little discussion with Mrs. Hunycutt."

The boys followed him around to the front and waited while he went inside. Mrs. Hunycutt met him and they could see them talking through the glass doors.

Suddenly Walter heard bicycle tires squealing behind him.

"Great," muttered Ralph, "the Friends of the Trees to the rescue."

He turned to see thirty or so Dinosaurs of all types on sturdy bikes, looking angry. They wore armbands.

Walter elbowed Ralph. "Maybe you had better take the bottle rack back to the laboratory before anything 'happens' to it," he suggested.

Ralph nodded and turned quietly to go.

"Just a minute, young saur," said the old lady Stegosaur Walter had met before, pointing her umbrella at Ralph. "Where do you think you are going with our friends?"

Ralph just kept tiptoeing off.

"Stop him, Henry!" the lady shouted, and banged her umbrella down on Henry's head.

Henry, a chubby Stegosaur kid, lumbered off his bike and bounded after Ralph. Ralph stayed just out of reach, but Henry managed to get a grip on the bottle rack. Ralph pulled it back and they struggled for it. Henry lost his grip and sat back on the sidewalk with a loud grunt. Ralph dashed up the library steps with the bottles and Walter stepped between him and the crowd.

"What are you doing with the lizards?" someone shouted.

Walter backed up to the steps of the library. He gulped, trying to think of something to stall the angry crowd of Dinosaurs creeping toward them.

Just then the Channel 8 Minicam Truck squealed up to the curb and a Dimetrodon with a portable TV camera got out. "Great," sighed Walter, trembling. "Now I'll be on the 6 o'clock news." He started sweating more.

Another Dinosaur, an Allosaur in a sport jacket, held out a microphone to the nearest Friend of the Trees and grinned into the camera. "You, saur, could you tell us the purpose of this demonstration?"

The Friend of the Trees looked surprised. He was a Triceratops. "Uh, well, these people are catching all the little animals in the park, and, uh, we didn't think that was right."

"Yes!" said the lady Dinosaur with the umbrella. "We do not want our natural environment disturbed!"

"And that goes for Dr. Krebnickel, too!" added Cora.

Just as Cora said that, Walter heard the library door open behind him. His heart thumped wildly when he saw that it was Dr. Heminglas. He must have still been researching and heard the commotion.

Heminglas stared at Walter, straightened his spotless white suit, and turned to the crowd and the camera.

"Look! It's Fairfax Heminglas!" someone shouted.

The TV camera quickly zoomed in on the celebrity. Heminglas help up one three-clawed hand for attention. "Friends of the Trees," he said in a gurgling voice, "the misguided Dr. Krebnickel is on the roof, harassing some defenseless reptile. But his pitiful captives are right here, in these bottles. You must save your lizard friends from certain extermination in some barbaric experiment!"

"Now just a minute!"

Ralph's voice rang out indignantly. He pushed his way past Dr. Heminglas. "Now just wait," he shouted. "We are from the . . . Krebnickel Lizard Protection Foundation. There is no harm at all in our collecting samples . . ."

Walter heaved a sigh of relief and stepped back a little. It was the first time that Dr. Heminglas' eyes weren't on him. Walter was sure he suspected something. One gooey clay horn was threatening to slide over his eye, and the helmet was slipping again.

Ralph rambled on about saving the lizards from a rare disease as the Minicam zeroed in on him. Meanwhile, traffic began slowing down. Then people pulled over to watch the crowd. At last a police patrol car appeared and two large Tyrannosaurs got out and made their way through the crowd, asking questions.

Ralph kept stalling. Walter hoped that Dr. Krebnickel had time to catch the lizard. ". . . and if you really are Friends of the Trees, we know you wouldn't want Teehalt Park to lose all its lizards to Tail Blight. That's why the KLPF is tracking down and dipping lizards here . . ."

"There he is!" someone shouted.

It was Dr. Krebnickel, still on top of the library. The lizard scuttled away from him and down the front face of the building.

"I'll be right there, boys," the Doctor shouted down. "Don't let him escape!"

Walter ran up to the door with the TV camera right behind him. He could hear the Stegosaur lady shrieking hysterically and one of the policemen saying, "Just the facts, Ma'am."

The other cop was trying to get the crowd to go away, but they were just moving up the steps more insistently. Dr. Krebnickel slipped out of the door and stood beside Walter and Ralph. He shot a sidelong burning glance at the dapper, fat Dr. Heminglas, who glowered back icily.

"Steady, boys. We have a little audience, but they shouldn't cause us much trouble. We've broken no laws. Straighten your helmet, Walter. Let's get this lizard and be gone."

The lizard crawled further down the wall. Walter held his breath.

"Excuse me, saur, but could I see some identification?" One of the Tyrannosaur officers stepped up to Dr. Krebnickel.

Dr. Krebnickel stuck the net under one arm and probed his baggy pants forgetfully for his wallet, mumbling to himself. Suddenly Dr. Heminglas stepped forward.

"You will not need to see the papers of the famous Dr. Krebnickel, surely," he wheedled sarcastically. "But you might ask him if he has a Wildlife Collecting Permit. Those lizards are city property."

The lizard inched further down the wall.

"Keep out of this, Fairfax," Dr. Krebnickel snapped.

"Protect our lizards!" screamed a Friend of the Trees, and the crowd moved forward a little.

"What are you really after?" Dr. Heminglass hissed, his green jowls quivering. "And what is the story on your very strangely attired small friend there?"

"Wouldn't you like to know?" Dr. Krebnickel growled, pushing.

The officer gingerly tried to get between the two scientists. "Just a minute," he said.

The lizard made its move. It scurried down the corner of the door frame and Walter snapped his net around it. The T.V camera, which had been filming Dr. Heminglas, whipped around and hit Walter right in the back of the helmet. It flew off and bounced noisily down the steps.

That was when the screaming started.

"His head came off! Look, Cora!"

"IT'S A HUMAN!" Henry the chubby Stegosaur squealed.

"It's horrible!" someone else shouted.

The policeman looked at Walter's eyes and pink skin beneath the smeared clay and fell backwards down the steps in terror.

"A Human!" Dr. Heminglass shouted. "I knew you were hiding something, Krebnickel."

Everybody was going crazy. It was a riot. Walter heard Ralph calling his name. Then he felt thorny fingers grab him and he was snatched off the steps.

"Stop!" he heard Dr. Krebnickel shout. "Officers, help! This is kidnapping. He's stealing Walter."

"There's no law against kidnapping *Humans*, Krebnickel," boomed out a loud voice above Walter. It was Dr. Heminglas. And his claws were so tight around Walter he could hardly breathe.

Then he was thrown into some cushions. A door slammed. Walter sat up in a daze. The TV camera was right next to him, filming him through a car window. The announcer was shouting excitedly.

"YousawitfirstrightonChannel8EyewitnessNews! AnactualHumanchildalive, somehowsurvivingtheages . . ."

Then Dr. Heminglas pressed the accelerator down and they sped swiftly away from Teehalt Park.

10 : *Dr. Heminglas*

WALTER was groggy from the accident, but as soon as he realized they were leaving Dr. Krebnickel, Ralph, and all the lizards, he started screaming. Dr. Heminglas looked around at him, his yellow cat's eyes narrowing. Walter screamed harder and tried to reach the doors, but his arms were pinned to his side. He was trapped. The worst had happened. Now he would never see his parents again. His voice rose as he kicked and flopped around.

"Silence, Human child," hissed Dr. Heminglas. He had a very wide Tyrannosaur smile with millions of shining teeth.

Walter's scream slowly faded and tapered off to a whimper.

"That's better," said Dr. Heminglas, flicking at a smudge on his black and white checked, perfectly tailored suit.

Walter discovered what was holding his arms. It was Heminglas' scaly green tail, wound about him in tight coils. Walter's heart turned into a floating pool of ice. There was no way to get free.

"Wonderful," Heminglas gurgled to himself. "I knew the old fool had something brewing. The fake tail made me suspicious. But I never imagined he actually had captured a Human." The warty green scales around his eyes puffed as he smiled. "Are you intelligent, monster?" he asked.

He tickled Walter under the nose with the tip of his tail to get a response. Walter surprised him by immediately grabbing the end of it in his mouth and chomping hard. Dr. Heminglas roared like a train trying to stop. The car swerved dangerously.

"When I'm treated intelligently," Walter replied as the Doctor released his hold. "And where I come from, you're the monster."

"Where you come from?" Dr. Heminglas' creepy eyes narrowed again as he licked his injured tail. "Are you a member of a lost tribe of Humans from some backward country?"

Walter didn't intend to give Dr. Heminglas any information at all. Still, maybe it would be better to talk to him a little. Walter didn't like the gleam of his long teeth, and didn't want to run the risk of being a snack.

"I'm from Fozbek," Walter said.

Dr. Heminglas' warty eyebrows went up. "Where's that?"

"Fozbek," Walter replied calmly, "is a planet which Earth scientists have not discovered yet. Except Dr. Krebnickel, of course. It's too small for your telescopes. It was founded millions of years ago by survivors of the Human race from Earth."

"And how did Krebnickel get you from this . . . Fozbek?" asked Dr. Heminglas, his eyes gleaming.

"Oh, a little box he has in his laboratory. I've been to your planet five times now." Walter was beginning to enjoy this.

"Then why were you in the park catching all the lizards?" Dr. Heminglas snarled.

"Ummmmm . . ."

"Do not play clever with me, little hairy beast! The lizards must be the crux of the matter. Don't you worry. I'll have the truth out of you. I have the means."

Walter gulped. Whatever "the means" was, it sounded nasty. They were passing through a very wealthy part of town very swiftly. Manors and mansions flashed past them, and golf courses and estates. At last Dr. Heminglas pulled up to a huge stone wall with iron gates. The gates, emblazoned with a big "H", slowly opened when Dr. Heminglas pushed a button next to the car radio. They drove past the entrance down a long cobbled road. There was a mansion on top of a hill. It was surrounded by immense evergreen trees.

"Just to make sure your friends don't follow you, I'm taking you to my private laboratory," Dr. Heminglas informed him.

He drove off the road and right up the lawn to a fir tree that was so huge the car pulled under its branches and stopped beside the trunk. Suddenly the area under the tree began to sink. It was a big round elevator in the lawn! Walter gulped. Dr. Krebnickel would never find him now. They traveled down several feet in the dark. Then they stopped and Dr. Heminglas drove the car into a tunnel. Walter watched the elevator go back up the tree behind them. In another moment they were inside a lighted drive-in laboratory under the ground.

The laboratory made Walter gasp. The black reptilian limousine cruised into a space in the brightly lit laboratory beside rows of embryos floating in jars. There was a little pink baby pig and an elephant and an aardvark. Their eyes looked sad.

Heminglas opened the door and pulled Walter out. He thought of running for the stairs at the end of the room, but decided the big Tyrannosaur would probably catch him. Besides, he didn't know where the stairs led.

Dr. Heminglas' laboratory was impressive, but it was the opposite of Dr. Krebnickel's. It had shiny new equipment, a flashy modern computer and slick rows of bottles, vials, and test tubes. But the main thing Walter noticed was the neatness. Everything was in rows or stacked or straightened. There were no dirty lab coats hanging over makeshift equipment as in Dr. Krebnickel's lab. No old pickle jars, no doughnut boxes.

Dr. Heminglas gave Walter a chair and turned to tidy up the only place in the lab that looked used. It was an area with lots of flasks and vials and a copper dish over a low bunsen flame. Stacks of notes and a couple of sandwich crusts lay beside it.

"Drat!" Dr. Heminglas muttered. "I should have cleaned this up before going to the library." He slid a roll of paper out of his coat and put it with the other papers.

Walter's jaw dropped. "You thief! That's one of Dr. Krebnickel's alchemy scrolls, and it's not supposed to leave the library."

Dr. Heminglas sneered, "Yes, and Hunycutt watches me like a hawk. Fortunately the disturbance you created outside the library afforded me a chance to lift it. It will be invaluable to my growth-rate experiments. Those old alchemists knew more than we give them credit for. I keep missing the right formula by only an ingredient or two. But now I have something more interesting to work on—you."

Dr. Heminglas rubbed his knobby three-clawed hands together. "Where to begin, where to begin? Perhaps I should make some tests to determine if you are truly a Human. Yes, yes, that would be the best starting point."

Heminglas took X-rays and clippings of his hair and nails to analyze. The part Walter liked least was the blood test. Finally, when Dr. Heminglas finished with the brain wave tests, and took off all the wires taped to Walter's head, he said in a snaky voice,

"You are a perfect specimen of a Human. Amazing."

"I could have told you that," Walter said.

"Silence. Are you still sticking by your 'Fozbek' story?"

"Until you come up with a better one," Walter said.

Dr. Heminglas fumed. "Oh, I shall discover Dr. Krebnickel's secret, don't you worry about that. Imagine, if I could get about a dozen of you creatures! I could build a park out near the airport and stock it with Humans. Human World, I could call it. It would be worth a fortune, and establish me as a great scientist." His eyes gleamed. "I know people who would lend me the money to build. All I have to do is show them you. I have friends, little monster. Yes, I have friends."

"*I* have friends," Walter said, "*you* have backers." He gripped the pebbly arms of his chair as he thought of himself stuck in a freak show forever while Dr. Heminglas got rich off him.

Heminglas ignored him, and began puttering with a big computer which ran along one wall. Walter eyed the door. But before he could make a break for it, Dr. Heminglas shoved him into a glass booth beside the computer banks. He strapped him in and closed the door. Switches were flipped and power surged through the computer. Buttons were pushed and strange lights came on in the booth. Dr. Heminglas began reading from a tape the machine was spewing out. He wrote something on a pad. The computer gurgled.

"So much for your 'Fozbek' story." Heminglas

glanced at him. "You are from Earth. There is no other explanation. But you have peculiar electromagnetic properties. You distort space oddly. I wonder if you are radioactive?"

He punched some more buttons and the computer whirred.

"Xenon!" Dr. Heminglas suddenly shouted. "I get a high and very strange reading of Xenon."

He peered inside the booth. His look made Walter's skin crawl.

"It must be! I remember Krebnickel working on some strange thing called the Krebnickel Principle, involving the vibratory rate of elements and space-time. You are from a parallel Earth!"

Walter sank back in the chair, defeated. Now he was lost.

"Yes, that's it, isn't it, my fine animal? Not a time machine or another planet, but another universe is the answer. You wait right there while I run upstairs and get my Portable Rare Gas Unit. And just in case, I'll get an injection of my own mixture of Truth Serum. There might be a lot you could tell me if I could loosen your tongue. And when I know how you got here, I'll be able to acquire more of your kind."

Dr. Heminglas giggled a sinister laugh and waddled through the forests of glass tubes and metallic contraptions festooning his laboratory. He clambered up the stairs, unlocked the metal door, and disappeared behind it. Walter caught a glimpse of sumptuous living quarters beyond.

Walter fought the urge to cry, but it was no use.

Things had just gone from terrible to ultra-terrible. The tears were hot and salty and he had to blink a lot since he couldn't wipe them away with his hands. After he cried a while he felt a little better.

He also decided he'd better try something even if there were no hope of escape. He tried wriggling his hands through the straps on the chair. He worked his right hand half under the strap even though it pinched him horribly. He closed his eyes and pulled hard. The strap budged ever so slightly.

Then he caught a tiny flicker of movement out of the corner of his eye. A fat green lizard was crawling down the edge of the car door. It had brown spots and a broken tail. It was the lost Xenon doorway lizard! It must have been tangled in the net when Walter was kidnapped. He wriggled his hands harder. If he could escape with the lizard, he still stood a chance of being transferred back to his world.

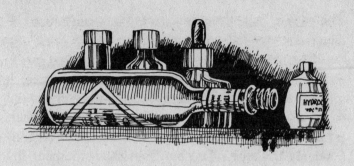

11: *The Missing Ingredient*

"DON'T you go anywhere, lizard," he said as he worked at the straps.

The lizard tilted its head and blinked at him. It jumped to the concrete floor with a faint plop.

"Stay there," Walter begged.

Unheeding, the lizard scuttled across the floor cautiously, pausing now and again to look for danger. It came to the edge of Heminglas' work table and dashed up it. Walter figured it was looking for a way out. He prayed it wouldn't find one before he could work his way free. His right hand was squished and pink, but he could feel it sliding a little.

The Xenon lizard rustled across Dr. Heminglas' neat stack of notes. It ran into the alchemy scroll as into a tunnel, emerging next to the dish of cooling growth-rate chemicals.

"Look out," Walter called, "that stuff could be dangerous."

The lizard paid no attention, but continued its exploration up a level to a shelf of chemical bottles. It scurried among the vials and tubes, darting in and out of the shadows. Apparently it decided to travel higher, for it stood on a fallen test tube to reach the next shelf. Suddenly the tube rolled out from under the poor lizard and both tumbled off the shelf directly onto the bowl of formula. The test tube shattered, spraying some red liquid over the spill where the bowl had been. It now lay smashed on the floor. The lizard got up and shook itself.

"Get out of there, lizard," Walter yelled, "Before you get poisoned."

The red liquid was doing something to the mixture. It was sizzling, and green smoke was rising from the spill. Walter moaned in horror as the lizard licked the stuff off its lips.

Walter felt sick. His only chance now was to get loose and get the lizard back to Dr. Krebnickel before the chemicals could hurt it. He couldn't believe how awful his luck was. Fear made his hand numb as he worked it against the strap.

The next time he looked up the lizard was rollicking along the shelf again, knocking vials of chemicals off left and right. The original spill was now obliterated with new liquids.

The lizard got to the lab wall and was climbing like a champion. Then, just when Walter had decided the chemicals had not hurt it, the lizard stopped moving. Walter held his breath. The lizard quivered a bit. Walter's heart froze. Then, with a shudder, the lizard . . . swelled.

Walter blinked. The lizard blinked too. It gave another tremor and puffed up even bigger. Walter couldn't believe his eyes. The lizard was now twice as big as it had been, all in proportion. It scampered a few feet up the wall before another series of quivers hit it and it enlarged again. The lizard was growing.

"Growth-rate experiments . . ." Walter muttered as he remembered the title of the scroll, ". . . *On Ye Alteration of Ye Animale Syze.* Holy Cow! That red stuff—it must have been the missing ingredient!"

At that moment Walter's hand popped free. He watched the rapidly expanding lizard creep onto a ceiling beam as he unbuckled the other straps, and pushed open the glass door. He was shaking with tension.

He was free, but he couldn't leave without the Xenon lizard. He tried coaxing it down with baby talk, but all he could see of it was a green paw the size of his own from around a beam. Every few seconds it would tremble and expand again. It must be as big as an alligator now.

Just then Dr. Heminglas came through the door carrying his Portable Rare Gas Unit and a black bag. His yellow eyes narrowed when he saw Walter. Walter just gave a sheepish grin and sort of waved.

"Ahhh," Dr. Heminglas said, "Very clever. Excellent. You are an extraordinary specimen, Fozbek. Now we shall find out who you are and where you really come from.''

He put the equipment beside him on the landing and extracted a fat metal syringe from the bag. Walter gulped and snuck a look at the Xenon lizard, apparently dozing on the rafter.

"Before you inject me with Truth Serum," said Walter shakily, "I think you should look up at that beam. Your growth-rate stuff worked. There's an eight foot lizard up there."

Dr. Heminglas chuckled as he filled the syringe. "Please, let's have none of that. Your tricks won't work."

Dr. Heminglas flicked the door closed behind him with his tail. The door slammed with a crash. Suddenly there was a scrambling sound above them and a great green streak leaped onto the floor. The lizard! It was the size of a cow.

Heminglas threw up his hands and screamed like a siren. The hypodermic clattered onto the floor. The lizard, confused by all the noise, ran up the stairs toward the scientist in a wallowing gallop. Heminglas howled in terror.

"The formula! It worked."

With one final hop the giant Xenon lizard plopped on the landing with Heminglas who uttered one short squeal and toppled over his own tail, crashing through the railing. He smashed into a stack of crates and lay in a green scaly mass, unconscious.

"Hooray!" Walter shouted to the lizard. "You did it, you knocked out Dr. Heminglas!"

The lizard cocked its head warily and blinked. Walter didn't think it understood, but he had been talking to reptiles all day and couldn't help talking to this one. It no longer looked alarmed, so he gently climbed the stairs, talking softly all the while.

"You're such a nice lizard. I bet you're strong, too. Yeah. Would you like to take me back to your park?"

He tenderly stroked its back and found that it was much softer than Ralph's. The lizard closed its eyes when he scratched it behind the head. And it . . . purred. Walter figured it was now or never, and he had only one plan. The lizard was too big for Walter to carry back to Teehalt Park, so it would have to carry him.

He straddled it slowly behind its front legs. It turned its head to look at him, but didn't flinch. He kept stroking it until he was safely saddled with his legs locked underneath. Then he swung the door open wide and nudged.

With a bolt they were off!

His reptilian steed dashed through the huge rooms of Dr. Heminglas' mansion, bounding off saurian furniture while Walter clung desperately. Game rooms and dining rooms flashed past. Finally they skidded around a corner and Walter glimpsed a long hall with a butler at the other end trying to climb up a curtain.

"Open the door!" Walter whooped like a cowboy.

The Dinosaur butler kicked the front door open as he continued mounting the curtain. A square of bright light flashed past and Walter and the lizard were out of the house and galloping down the rolling green lawn. Walter just hung on for dear life and hoped the lizard went the right way.

The Xenon lizard took the brick wall around Heminglas' property in a single jarring bound, and then they were off down the road at a steady clip. Walter could see amazed Dinosaur faces flash past inside cars. Dinosaur buildings wobbled by. He saw that they were coming to an intersection ahead, with cars and buses and pedestrians. He closed his eyes and hugged the lizard tight.

Car brakes squealed, he heard a crash or two. Dinosaur horns began honking. Shoppers were screaming.

"Look out!"

"Mama, what is it?"

"A . . . HUMAN!"

At the mention of the word "Human" pandemonium broke out. The lizard zigged and zagged through the screaming crowd. Walter almost felt proud it was "his" lizard. He realized it had been dodging birds and cats all of its life. It was pretty brave.

At last the sounds of panic faded and Walter opened his eyes. Trees and shrubs sped past in a blur. They were bounding down a back alley, then across a

couple of yards. An Allosaur hopped over his lawn mower to avoid them. His shriek was so pitiful Walter nearly laughed. He couldn't believe all these fearsome Dinosaurs could be afraid of a big lizard and a small Human. He was beginning to feel a little brave also, with his silly disguise off. Now he could confront the Dinosaur world as Walter Fozbek, Human. That didn't sound so frightening anymore.

Then, there it was ahead of them—Teehalt Park. Walter nearly cheered for the lizard's accuracy. It bounded onto the grassy slope and stopped just in front of some frisbee players, panting. Walter sat up and looked at a startled Iguanodon. The unheeded frisbee bonked it right in the head.

Walter held up his little pink Human claws and snarled. The Iguanodons ran off making terrified honking noises, their tails bobbing behind them. Walter nearly fell off his lizard laughing. Of course! Dinosaurs would be just as afraid of a Human as Humans would be of a Dinosaur. Then he heard footsteps in the grass behind him and swiveled to put on another show.

"Dr. Krebnickel! Ralph!"

His friends stood gaping at the giant lizard. "How . . ." Dr. Krebnickel began.

"Not now," Walter said, suddenly remembering his predicament. "Help me talk this lizard into following us back to the lab. It's the Xenon lizard. I'll explain later."

As the afternoon sun shone through the treetops,

three figures could be seen coaxing a strange shape across Mars Road. Fortunately, there were no cars traveling down that road, and the only witnesses, some ancient Pterodactyl ladies in adjoining houses refused to believe what they had seen, preferring to blame their glasses.

12 : *A Reducing Course*

"REMARKABLE," Dr. Krebnickel kept repeating, "Remarkable. So those old scrolls did have some secrets after all."

The Xenon lizard looked up from his meal of cat food and lettuce and blinked. They had managed to get it into Dr. Krebnickel's kitchen with the smelly concoction.

"I guess so," Walter sighed. He had explained as best he could about Dr. Heminglas' lab and the growth-rate experiments and the red liquid and his escape. They had all laughed when he told them how Dr. Heminglas was so afraid of the lizard that he fell off the stairs.

Ralph chuckled. "Dr. Heminglas will have lots of reporters' questions to answer when he wakes up. He was the one who left with you, after all."

"Omigosh," Walter started. "What happened at the library after I was kidnapped?"

Ralph shrugged. "Oh, more panic. The policeman was so scared he just got in his car and drove off in the opposite direction. The Channel 8 people asked Dr. Krebnickel a lot of questions, but he wouldn't say anything."

"Yes," Dr. Krebnickel mumbled as he made measurements of the lunching lizard. "I just told them I would have a statement to make later."

"What are you going to tell them?" Walter asked.

"Mass hypnosis, I suppose, brought about by the hysterical Friends of the Trees. You appeared to be an extinct animal because the crowd was possessed with the idea of extinction. Simple hallucination, I guess." He sighed. "I haven't really decided what to tell them."

"But they took pictures of Walter," Ralph objected.

"Let's hope they are poor pictures, then," said Dr. Krebnickel. "But for now, could you boys help me get this specimen into the lab? I want to take some precise measurements . . ."

"Dr. Krebnickel," Ralph interrupted impatiently, "have you forgotten about Walter? It's nearly five-thirty. His parents will be at my house to pick him up soon."

"Oh, yes," Dr. Krebnickel smiled forgetfully. "I forgot about today's primary marvel."

Walter grinned. "Can I go back now? I mean, now that we have the right lizard, all I have to do is look at him through the glasses, right?"

Dr. Krebnickel's duck-billed smile faded. "I don't know, Walter. With this lizard as he was when you saw him, yes. But now, this big . . . the chemicals might have changed his molecular . . ."

Walter felt tears welling up. He couldn't have come this far for nothing. His parents . . .

"Wake him up," Ralph snorted.

They all looked at him dumbly.

"Quarwyn," Ralph insisted. "Wake him up again. He's the only one who can solve this."

Dr. Krebnickel gulped as though he had been ordered to wake a dragon. But he had no other answer, so he slowly led the giant Xenon lizard downstairs with the plate of goo as lure. Walter followed, blinking back tears.

"I—I've never disturbed him three times in one day," Dr. Krebnickel hesitated.

"Just turn him on," Walter pleaded.

Dr. Krebnickel closed his eyes and flipped the switch. Lights flickered and raced up the giant crystals, but Quarwyn did not speak.

"This had better be good," it said quietly after a while.

Dr. Krebnickel stepped back to let its sensors scan the huge lizard.

"Strange," the computer buzzed. "There seems to be some malfunction in my sensors."

"Your sensors are fine," Walter explained.

"This is my Xenon doorway back to the other universe. It accidentally ate some of Dr. Heminglas' growth-rate formula after some strange red liquid spilled . . ."

"QUARWYN DOES NOT WISH TO HEAR MORE!" the computer sputtered.

"But can you help?" Dr. Krebnickel ventured. "We have little time left."

"Quarwyn can help. Place a biopsy of the mutant beast in Quarwyn's analysis box."

"Oh, dear," Dr. Krebnickel muttered.

"What does he mean?" Ralph queried.

"A sample of the animal's tissue," Dr. Krebnickel replied, eyeing the giant lizard nervously. "But where to take it from and how to take it is a different question."

"Try the tail," Quarwyn commented drily.

Walter stroked the lizard's back gently while Ralph gingerly—very gingerly—scraped off some brittle scales from its tail stump into a cup. The lizard looked around casually like a cow observing its milker.

Dr. Krebnickel placed the scrapings in a cleaned pickle jar which went in a niche in Quarwyn's crystal bank.

"Very good," the computer commented, then went silent as yellow lights chased blue shadows over its crystals. After a few moments, Quarwyn glowed pinkly. "Yes. Simple, actually. Krebnickel, fetch the following ingredients: Trisodium Phosphate, 2 gr.; Einsteinium, 1 dram mixed in 12 cc's H_2SO_4 . . ."

Quarwyn continued rattling off the recipe while

poor Dr. Krebnickel dashed about the lab gathering armloads of old Worcestershire sauce bottles and butter tubs filled with chemicals. This made the lizard nervous. It forgot about its lunch and began looking for the way out. It seemed to Walter it had had enough excitement for one day, too. He headed it off and calmed it down by stroking its head and murmuring softly. At last Quarwyn's list seemed to end, and Dr. Krebnickel measured the last item into a box on the computer's side.

"But where's the red liquid, the key ingredient?" asked Walter, puzzled.

"Not required yet," Quarwyn replied. "Quarwyn must heat this mixture to 400° K under a little pressure first. Krebnickel can search for the missing ingredient meanwhile."

"But what is it?" Dr. Krebnickel asked timidly.

"An acid formed from the fermented juice of an herb with a little salt added. Tabasco sauce, by name. It seems Dr. Heminglas likes to snack in his laboratory."

Walter whooped with laughter. Fat old Dr. Heminglas would never guess what the missing ingredient was!

"Good grief, I don't think I have any," said Dr. Krebnickel and rushed off upstairs.

Walter tried to calm the lizard while Ralph giggled, "Poor Dr. Heminglas!"

Dr. Krebnickel returned shortly, panting. "Mrs. Packeltide next door had some, but she looked at me most queerly," he clucked.

Two dashes into Quarwyn's box, a flickering of lights, and the machine deposited a grey trickle into a jelly glass underneath it.

"Done," said Quarwyn. "I have altered it slightly to reverse the growing process. It should shrink to normal. Now, Doctor, I am going back to slumberland. I will not be speaking to you for several days, understood?"

"But—"

"GOOD NIGHT," Quarwyn thundered. "Goodby, Human Walter. Have a nice trip." The computer's lights faded to a pale twinkle.

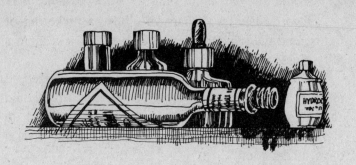

13: *Back Again*

WALTER held the lizard's head up and rubbed its neck while Dr. Krebnickel poured the formula down its throat. He was surprised how peacefully it accepted the drink, but he figured it was pretty tired of fighting. They stood back and watched it tremble and shrink, tremble and shrink, reversing the process Walter had watched at Dr. Heminglas' lab. Soon it was the size of a normal lizard and Dr. Krebnickel had it strapped securely into a little wire device on the table.

"Are you sure you can't spare a few moments for some X-rays?" Dr. Krebnickel pleaded.

Walter shook his head violently. "Please, let's try before anything else can go wrong."

"I see what you mean." Dr. Krebnickel sighed and reluctantly picked up the Xenon glasses. "I had *so* wanted to record this event properly. At any rate, it has been a privilege to know you, Walter Fozbek. You are a credit to your species.''

"Thank you, Doc," Walter said softly. He turned and shook Ralph's stumpy grey hand. "And thank you, Ralph. I don't think I could have gotten further than your living room if it hadn't been for you. You're the best cousin I've got, in any world."

Ralph gulped with emotion and pumped Walter's hand. "It's been a real adventure today, Walter. Give my best to the other me."

They all laughed nervously.

Dr. Krebnickel stepped forward awkwardly with the spectacles. "I've wired them into the Neutrino Turbine so you will pass through far more rapidly than you did last night. It should be instantaneous. Good-bye, Walter."

He put the Xenon spectacles over Walter's eyes. The lizard looked like a bright green snowflake behind the faceted lens. Dr. Krebnickel stepped behind the curtain. Walter felt tingly all over. He closed his eyes tightly. Then, suddenly, he could no longer feel his body. It was as though he were falling through space. Then the feeling passed. He opened his eyes.

"Hello, Walter," Dr. Krebnickel smiled. He was pink and had white hair and a nose. No bill or claws or pebbly green skin. No tail. And there was the Human Ralph.

"Dr. Krebnickel! Ralph! I'm back!"

They all hugged and jumped around.

"There," said Dr. Krebnickel, "we've done it and it isn't even 7 o'clock."

"What's that on your face?" Ralph wondered. "And look at his clothes, Dr. Krebnickel."

"Oh," said Walter, wiping his cheek. "That's clay. Had to get made up to look like a Triceratops. These are the other Walter's clothes." He kept looking back and forth. "You both look so good, I can't believe it. I never would have thought just the sight of another Human could be this neat."

Ralph laughed. "You look better without horns, too. Listen, why don't we all go upstairs and watch the 7 o'clock news and have some tea before we go home?"

"And cookies," said Walter. He was very hungry. It had been a long day since that strange Dinosaur breakfast.

They all went into Dr. Krebnickel's study. Walter snuggled down into a thickly stuffed chair. It was soft and proportioned for Humans. The news came on the very large TV screen (Dr. Krebnickel had built it) and the "riot" at Teehalt Park was coming up. They sipped and watched.

Anchorman Dave Andrews narrated: "An incident at Teehalt Park Branch Library today had local environmental groups, the Sheriff's Department, and museum curators in an uproar. I was at the scene with our Channel 8 Minicam when . . ."

The Minicam film showed Dr. Krebnickel and two kids dressed up to look like Dinosaurs standing at the top of the library steps, surrounded by a crowd of protesters. Then the camera was on Dr. Krebnickel talking to a policeman, then something bumped into the camera and by the time it stopped wobbling around all that could be seen was the back of a man in a spotless white suit carrying something to a car. Whatever he was carrying had a tail. Then the camera showed a close-up shot of a strange looking kid in the dark back seat of a car. Then it drove away.

"Attempts to reach Dr. Heminglas have been unsuccessful, and Dr. Krebnickel has offered no explanation for what happened today. Now for the latest on that train derailment, we go to Betty Coy . . ."

Dr. Krebnickel turned down the sound.

"That was the Dinosaur me," Walter said.

"Yes. Dressed up to look like a Human disguised as a Dinosaur."

Ralph chuckled. "I fixed him up this morning with construction paper and clay over his horns. Then he did me up like a Dinosaur. We told my folks we were going to a Dinosaur Festival here and had to go in costume."

"That's it!" Dr. Krebnickel announced, and he ran to the telephone.

Ralph and Walter exchanged puzzled glances as he dialed.

"Hello? Channel 8? This is Ladislav Krebnickel, and I'm ready to talk about what happened at Teehalt Park today." Dr. Krebnickel winked while they hooked up his call to Dave Andrews' desk so that Dr. Krebnickel could talk on the air.

"Yes. Mr. Andrews? Our little demonstration today was an attention-getter for an exciting event to benefit the Children's Museum. Dr. Heminglas has asked me to join him in sponsoring a Dinosaur Festival at Teehalt Park next week. Everyone is invited to come dressed as their favorite Dinosaur. Dr. Heminglas will judge the costumes and there will be prizes . . . Oh, and Dr. Heminglas has generously offered to buy a new Dinosaur skeleton for the Children's Museum in honor of the occasion. Thank you for donating time on your telecast."

Dr. Krebnickel hung up. Dave Andrews was looking at his phone in an odd sort of way. The sound was turned up.

"WDIN, Channel 8 television is of course proud to donate some of our air time to this . . . uh . . . worthwhile cause. Now for the explosion in Madrid . . ."

Dr. Krebnickel turned the set off and they all laughed. When Walter caught his breath he said, "Wait until Dr. Heminglas hears that he's sponsoring a Dinosaur Festival. And when they tell him he's shelling out for a new skeleton, he'll explode!"

"Yes, he will be very angry, Fairfax will," Dr. Krebnickel nodded. "But he won't back out. It would be embarrassing to the business world if he refused now. And he must keep up his image with them."

The phone rang just then and Dr. Krebnickel answered it. "Hello. Yes, he's here, Mrs. Fozbek, would you like to speak with him? Oh. Of course I will. Goodbye." He hung up. "That was Ralph's mother. Supper's waiting for you."

Walter swallowed a mouthful of cookies. It sure would be good to see Mom and Dad again. He and Ralph waited on the front porch while Dr. Krebnickel went back downstairs. All the houses and cars were back to their good old Human dimensions. Soon Dr. Krebnickel stepped out into the evening air with them, holding the Xenon lizard squirming between two fingers. Walter looked closely at it. It was almost the same as the one in the Dinosaur universe. It blinked at him.

"I think it's time we freed our little friend," Dr. Krebnickel said.

It looked at Walter in a very unlizardlike way for a moment, then slithered out of the Doctor's grasp. It scampered down the steps and across the street. The sun was low and when the lizard paused at the edge of the grass to look back, orange and yellow flashed off its eyes.

"Well, boys," Dr. Krebnickel said, "enjoy your supper. I have to go inside and inspect my Xenon spectacles thoroughly. I really can't thank you enough for finding them, Walter."

There was a big lump in Walter's throat. He found he couldn't even manage to say thank you to Dr. Krebnickel. He would still be stranded in the other universe if not for him. He and Ralph turned and walked down the sidewalk.

"Oh, yes, and boys," Dr. Krebnickel shouted, leaning out around a post, "don't forget to work on your costumes. We're going to have a Dinosaur Festival, remember!"

They headed home slowly, then, glancing at each other, they broke into a trot. They ended up running a full-fledged race back to Aunt Alice's house. As Walter bounced into the front yard he saw his parents' clunky old blue station wagon and his heart gave a flutter. His mother and father were leaning against it talking to Uncle Albert. They were all pink and smooth with not a horn in sight.

He had never been so happy in his life.

"Whoa," his father said as Walter squeezed him, "we've only been gone a week. You'll bend my glasses."

"You sure look better than you did this morning in that Dinosaur get-up," Uncle Albert snorted.

Walter grinned. "I sure feel better, too."

14 : *The Dinosaur Festival*

WALTER tried to scratch his itching nose, but there was too much clay on it. He straightened the horn over his left eye, which was beginning to loosen from his sweating. The Dinosaur costume made him anxious.

"Don't worry," Ralph whispered. "You look great."

"So do you," Walter whispered back, and giggled. Actually, in this world Ralph made a crummy Triceratops. He had a construction paper frill and a papier maché beak which had started to slip in the bright sunshine.

There were hundreds of Dinosaurs in Teehalt Park again, milling about or swinging or playing frisbee. There were paper Trachodons and clay Triceratopses and cardboard Stegosaurs. Walter smiled. There was a kid flying a Pteranodon kite. The Friends of the Trees even attended, with a boothful of ladies warning of Human extinction. (Such a silly thought!) Dr. Heminglas' Dinosaur Festival was the hit of the city.

But as he sat on the grass sipping grape Kool-aid Walter's thoughts couldn't help drifting back to that other world. Were they having a Human Festival? Was the other Walter sitting on the grass there wearing a pink furry suit? It made him chuckle.

Dr. Heminglas made him chuckle, too. He was standing with Dr. Krebnickel at the refreshment table, surrounded by a crowd of mothers. He was the most famous person there, and he had to act nice to them. He was sipping Kool-aid and shooting nasty glances at Dr. Krebnickel. Dr. Heminglas was dressed in another spotless white suit, but there were crossed band-aids on his bald head, probably from his fall from the stairs.

When they had first arrived to help Dr. Krebnickel set up the tables and the microphone and stuff, Dr. Heminglas had been livid with anger. He had hissed through clenched teeth, "Krebnickel, I know you hoped I would back out and ruin my standing in the community, but I spoiled your little plan, didn't I?" Then he added, "But I'll get even with you."

"Tsk, tsk, tsk," Dr. Krebnickel clucked, a twinkle in his eye, "then you would never find out what I did with the Dinosaur child . . ."

Dr. Heminglas turned purple with rage.

". . . or what the missing ingredient to your growth formula is."

Dr. Heminglas clenched his hands and stalked off speechless.

"MAY I HAVE YOUR ATTENTION PLEASE."

Walter's daydream was interrupted by the microphone's static voice. It was Dr. Heminglas.

"I AM READY TO ANNOUNCE THE WINNERS IN THE DINOSAUR COSTUME CONTEST. WOULD ALL CONTESTANTS PLEASE COME TO THE REFRESHMENT STAND."

All the cardboard Dimetrodons and plastic Tyrannosaurs came trooping. Walter and Ralph went too. There were about fifty contestants, and they lined up with their numbers on like draftees from the Paleozoic Era.

"VERY WELL," said Dr. Heminglas. "WE HAVE MADE OUR DECISION. FIRST PLACE GOES TO . . . NUMBER 12, SECOND PLACE TO NUMBER 15."

Ralph and Walter looked at each other, astounded. Walter was 12, and Ralph was 15. They had won first and second prize. Trembling with excitement, they went to stand with the other winners.

"AND YOU ARE . . ." Dr. Heminglas held out the microphone.

"WALTER FOZBEK," he said nervously.

At the sound of his name Dr. Heminglas blushed and looked at him very peculiarly.

"WELL, WALTER, IT LOOKS LIKE YOU HAVE HAD SOME PRACTICE BEING A TRICERATOPS. YOU EVEN HAVE NICE DINOSAUR CLOTHES."

TYRANNOSAUR

TRICERATOPS

PTERODACTYL

TRACHODON

ANKYLOSAUR

STEGOSAUR

DIMETRODON

CORYTHOSAUR

STYRACOSAUR

DRYPTOSAUR

Walter shrugged and accepted the box that was first prize. He went and stood by Dr. Krebnickel.

"Congratulations, my boy," Dr. Krebnickel said, winking, "you really do have the best disguise."

Ralph trotted over to join them, his prize under his arm. It was a beautiful stuffed Triceratops. Walter complimented him on it.

"Thanks," said Ralph, "but your prize is much nicer."

Walter suddenly looked down. He hadn't even looked at his prize. It was a big box covered with plastic wrap. It had a picture of mountains and caves and palm trees on it covered with brightly colored Dinosaurs of all sorts. Across the top was written: Your Very Own—DINOSAUR WORLD.

A CAST OF CHARACTERS
TO DELIGHT THE HEARTS
OF READERS!

BUNNICULA   **69252-X/$2.50**
James and Deborah Howe, illustrated by Alan Daniel
The now-famous story of the vampire bunny, this ALA
Notable Book begins the light-hearted story of the
small rabbit the Monroe family find in a shoebox at
a Dracula film. He looks like any ordinary bunny to
Harold the dog. But Chester, a well-read and observant
cat, is suspicious of the newcomer, whose teeth
strangely resemble fangs...

HOWLIDAY INN   **69294-5/$2.50**
James Howe, illustrated by Lynn Munsinger
"Another hit for the author of BUNNICULA!"
                                    School Library Journal
The continued "tail" of Chester the cat and
Harold the dog as they spend their summer vacation
at the foreboding Chateau Bow-Wow, a kennel run
by a mad scientist!

THE CELERY STALKS AT MIDNIGHT   69054-3/$2.50
James Howe, illustrated by Leslie Morrill
Bunnicula is back and on the loose in this third
hilarious novel featuring Chester the cat, Harold
the dog, and the famous vampire bunny. This time
Bunnicula is missing from his cage, and Chester
and Harold turn sleuth to find him, and save the
town from a stalk of bloodless celery!
"Expect surprises. Plenty of amusing things happen."
                            The New York Times Book Review

AV☾N Camelot Paperbacks